LIVIN'
MOVIN'
AND
HAVIN'
MY BEING
BY GOLLY

A JOURNEY
BY
URSULA McCAFFREY HEUISER

Order this book online at www.trafford.com
or email orders@trafford.com

Most Trafford titles are also available at major online book retailers.

Print information available on the last page.

ISBN: 978-1-4251-8572-5 (sc)

Cover Design: The Istock Store

Trafford rev. 10/21/2022

Trafford www.trafford.com
PUBLISHING

North America & international
toll-free: 844-688-6899 (USA & Canada)
fax: 812 355 4082

TABLE OF CONTENTS

DEDICATION

Without hesitation and barely missing the next beat of my heart, I must dedicate this expose of my heritage and life to our Heavenly Father. He is the very One who created this Ursula girl in the first place. I can't thank you enough, Heavenly Father, for this life, for I am created in Your image and likeness. Not a day goes by that I don't stop and offer you praise and thanksgiving. Sitting here in the peace and quiet of my Mountain Home, I raise my heart to you with love. It seems to me that you are a Father to me at each precious moment of my life. Thank you so much. You know all things; You know me better than I know myself, and oh, my goodness, how You love me. Thank you for loving me into existence. Your gift to me is my life and my gift back to you IS this life. Abe Lincoln once said, "If we know who we are and wither we go tethering, then maybe we will know how to get there". Well, it seems to me I've had a lot of tethering posts in my life and I thank God for every one of them.

This story takes me up to when I left home in 1956 with the exception of the last years of my Mother and Father. The next tethering post takes place with the Medical Mission Sisters. My Mom saved 110 of my letters from Africa so I will share those in my next story.

Now, I really have to thank St. Patrick, Apostle of Ireland. He is the one who brought the good news of God, the Father's Son, Jesus my Redeemer and His Holy Spirit to Ireland. It was there that my great grandfather, Patrick O'Brien, and great grandmother, Johanna Quinlan O'Brien, and great grandfather, John Charles McCaffrey, and great grandmother, Susan Harris, embraced the faith and passed it on. This faith that I have is like the air I breathe.

THE PRECIOUS PRESENT MOMENT

I have always been glued to the precious present moment. It is what God gives me right now, so, the now is very important to me. The next breath I take is the continuation of God's presence in my very soul. Of course the problems of life crowd in sometimes. God's Providence rises before the dawn. My mom used to say that our so called problems are not problems at all, but opportunities. You have to look them square in the face and change the situation if possible, or carry on and in due course things will get resolved.

I remember that my dad would say that a certain situation was like an albatross around one's neck. It took me years before I figured out what in the world the albatross is! Well, the albatross is that large web-footed sea bird. Wow! What a burden to have that creature hanging around one's neck.

Meanwhile, that next breath in the precious moment takes place. I love You, my God, and I will never cease to carry You in my heart. St. Alphonsus Liguori once said, "There is a practice that is most powerful in keeping us united with God. That practice is the constant recollection of His presence."

I would like to quote from Mother Angelica's little book of life's lessons:

"Here is a sentence we forget entirely: "Tomorrow will take care of itself." Why? Because tomorrow will soon be now. Have you ever noticed that there really is never a tomorrow? It's always NOW. Your whole life is now. Every moment of life is like God saying, Look, I know you messed up the last moment, but here's a new one. Every moment you breathe, God's power envelops you and sustains you in existence. Every instant of your life is brand new – you make it old by living in the past. And you make it a dream world by living in the future. So don't look back, because in order to look back you have to stop moving forward. The Father in Heaven has an awesome attribute. Everything is now for the Father, there is no past, no future with God; everything is now. Your prayer life is twenty-four hours a day. You fill up at meditation in your prayer time when you talk to Jesus, and then you and Jesus go out into the world moment by moment. You don't live in yesterday and you don't live in tomorrow."

My favorite passage from the Bible is "Be still and know that I am your God." (Ps. 46:10) It is in the stillness of the present moment that God wants me to acknowledge Him.

Here I am now a grandmother in these present moments writing memories of my life. Somebody once wrote, "A story is where the heart surprises the head." So we shall see what surprises are ahead. At this stage I am on the road to wrinkleville but there are no wrinkles in my heart! "If wrinkles must be written upon our brows, let them not be written upon the heart. The spirit should never grow old."

PROLOGUE

I want to let you know where this idea came from. Why write about my life?

You know there are very few big families left. My parents and grandparents didn't talk much about their growing up days. I began thinking about my own children, and then about their children and so on. Therefore, a great desire welled up in my heart to write this story. I must honor this desire, mainly to take time to thank God for my life and to preserve its history.

I cared for my mother for a few years; she lost her speech from a stroke. Ever since that time, when she could no longer speak, this desire to tell my story was born and has sprouted to fruition.

I read a historical novel once about a 14th century maiden who could neither read nor write. This was common in those days, but she was bursting with a desire to write a story, so she slipped out unbenounced to her parents, and casually made her way up the narrow cobblestone road to the Monastery. In front sat the Brother of Letters who would transcribe messages for the townsfolk. She explained her dilemma and he offered to write her story. She couldn't stay very long each time. She would hide the rolled up parchment under her long flowing robe and place it under loose stones around her fireplace in her bedroom. You may ask where am I going with this? You see, I had such admiration for that character. Look at what she went through to tell her story. I am capable without any obstacles to tell my own story and so I shall.

Now it is like I have a swarm of thoughts humming through my head just waiting to be written down.

MY HERITAGE

THE O'BRIEN'S

*I*t's great fun to look back at the folks who came before me. I will extract some information from a report prepared by my cousin, Neil O'Brien. Neil got most of his information from Aunt Dorothy.

I think I will begin with my great great grandfather on my mother's side, William O'Brien. In 1842, he left the city of Cork, Ireland, with his wife (I do not know her name) and nine children. However, Patrick O'Brien, my future great grandfather, had some sort of eye disease, and stayed behind at age one, to be raised by William's brother. Patrick was born March 17, 1841.

William and family arrived in New Orleans in 1842 during a yellow fever epidemic, which caused his death along with his wife and two of his children. The remaining six children were placed in an orphanage in New Orleans. Their names were, Mary, Kate, John, Dennis, Nora and Paul.

Patrick O'Brien, now 19, kept in contact with his brothers and sisters in America. He was raised on a sheep farm in County Cork, Ireland. He did not go to school because his aunt and uncle wanted him to continue speaking Gaelic, and the school required him to learn and speak English. They would have none of it so he remained on the farm.

He saved his money for passage to America in 1860, and landed in New York. He worked there a few months to get enough money to proceed closer to Galveston, where his sister Ellen lived. After several other jobs he finally arrived in Galveston and worked there for a year. Then, he joined his brother David in Austin and worked there for several years. David went on to Portland, Oregon, so Patrick got a job in Houston where he worked on the Houston and Texas Central Railroad, being built from Houston to Dallas. The railroad ran out of money when it reached Hutchins, Texas, and Patrick had to quit. He was so close to Dallas that he went there, bought hay bailing machinery, and contracted to bale hay for farmers in and around Dallas. There were approximately 3,000 people living in Dallas at that time. Eventually, the H & TC Railroad reached Union Terminal in Dallas on July 16, 1872.

Now, I want you to meet my lovely great grandmother Johannah Quinlan, born in Cork, Ireland, December 1, 1852. She was the 3rd oldest in a family of six girls and four boys. Her mother, Marry Anne Mannix Quinlan died at the age of 42. Johannah's father, Michael, left his children and sailed across the ocean to America . He left money with a banker to care for the children for two years. His goal was to send for them gradually.

Great great grandfather Michael Quinlan worked as a section foreman for a railroad. He founded the city, named for him, of Quinlan, Texas, east of Dallas. He then secured passage for his oldest daughter, Mary, but she wanted to marry an Englishman, so my great grandmother, Johannah, age 19, used her ticket. In 1871, Johannah sailed to New York and from there to Galveston, Texas, and by H & TC Railroad to Dallas, then by horse and buggy to Quinlan Texas. What courage and stamina she had. I'm sure her guardian angel was right beside her every step of the way!

Three younger sisters, Nora, Bridget and Elizabeth finally joined her. Nora and Bridget married in Dallas. Elizabeth died at age 18 of pneumonia. Johannah had brothers, John who died in infancy, Thomas who remained in Ireland with Sin Fein and James and Joseph who both worked in a bank. James, Joseph and John are all buried in Cork.

Johannah's two sisters, Mary and Ellen, did not come to America. Mary married Canute and moved to England where

2

both are buried. Ellen married James Foley of Cork. They had three girls, Anne, Elizabeth and Nora, and two sons, Joseph and William.

Johannah moved to Dallas around 1873, and served as a governess and tutor for the daughter of a Mr. Collins. She had been a governess for a child of a Lord in England. She met Patrick O'Brien in 1879 and they were married on March 1, 1880 at Sacred Heart Cathedral in Dallas, which was then located at Bryan St. There were approximately 15,000 people living in Dallas at that time.

Living on a modest farm located on land that later became in part Ross Avenue, three children were born to Patrick and Johannah, William Patrick , David Michael, and Marie Elizabeth – (my grandmother). In 1885, Patrick and Johannah moved to Hebron in Denton County, Texas, where Patrick leased some land. He resumed the hay bailing business. Seven more children followed: Ellen Josephine , Reginald Joseph (Uncle Monk) , Francis Charles (Uncle Frank) , Christopher Alphonso, Jeanette Margarite , Justin Dennis (Uncle Dennis) , Dorothy Clara (Aunt Dorothy) .

Johannah's father, Michael, came to Hebron and died there in 1898 at the age of 81. He was interred in the old Calvary Cemetery on Hall Street.

In 1903, Patrick purchased a farm about three miles SE of Lewisville. He raised cattle and cut timber. My cousin, Neal O'Brien, sent us a picture of Grandma & Grandpa O'Brien on their farm with all their kids and their 3 mules.

Uncles Monk, Frank and Dennis went to Holy Trinity High School in Dallas and college at the University of Dallas on Oak Lawn. The girls, except Jeanette, went to Ursuline Academy in Dallas founded in 1874.

And so the story continues....It so happened that Frank, Jeanette, Dennis and Dorothy were taken from Hebron to Sacred Heart Church in Rowlett to be baptized. It was a whole day trip by buggy. Grandpa Patrick could not afford to lose 2 days work so he waited until the weather would not permit any

3

work. The Priest said he would baptize the 3 younger children but Frank was too old to be baptized without any instructions. He didn't know that Grandma Johannah had been instructing the children every Sunday. She insisted that Frank was well-prepared in his faith. Still, the Priest refused to baptize him. Grandma told the priest, well, if you won't baptize Frank, there are a lot of protestant clergymen up near Hebron who want to. Needless to say, Frank indeed was baptized.

There was a Christian Church down the road from the farm. Grandma agreed to help the pastor out. Every Sunday, she sent one of her kids down the road to ring the church bell for the pastor.

About the year 1901, a Catholic priest was on his way from Sacred Heart Cathedral in Dallas to Denton, Texas. He rode a bicycle. It was getting dark so he stopped at the O'Brien farm and asked to spend the night. Grandma Johannah wasn't sure he was a priest, so she made him sit on the porch until Grandpa came home. He turned out to be legit and stayed for supper and then to spend the night. After supper, he offered to hear everyone's confessions. Johannah declined. She told him it had been 25 years since she had been to confession and she may have lost her faith. Later that evening Johannah was showing the priest to the bedroom – it was Patrick and Johannah's bedroom. She opened the door and held a lamp to light his way in. She looked up and she saw the Blessed Mother holding the Baby Jesus pass from one corner of the room and out the opposite side. She then asked the priest to hear her confession.

Grandpa Patrick passed away July 7, 1913, at the age of 62. He was also interred at the old Calvary Hill Cemetery. Johannah sold the Lewisville farm in 1915 and purchased 177 acres in Hutchins, Texas. Uncle Will moved there and farmed that land until he retired in 1951. Meanwhile, Johannah moved in 1915, to Dallas at 1924 Haskell Street. From there she moved to 121 Brooklyn Avenue in Oak Cliff. In 1927 she moved to 3707 Gilbert Avenue, one block from Holy Trinity Church, where she lived the rest of her life. This is where we all would drop in to visit.

GREAT GRANDFATHER PATRICK
O'BRIEN

GREAT GRANDMOTHER
JOHANNAH QUINLAN O'BRIEN

Grandmother O'Brien retained her Gaelic accent. She was a member of the 3rd Order of St. Francis, abstaining from meat on Wednesdays and Saturdays. On stormy nights, true to her Irish culture, she sprinkled Holy Water on everyone's pillow. She was a woman of great faith. She did not drink alcohol, but is reported to have a half-pint behind the picture of the great grandchildren "in the event she had a sinking spell." She kept a small safe beside her chair in the bedroom. She always sat by the front upstairs window. When we would visit, we could always see her up there as we got out of the car and waved to her. Upon entering the room you just wanted to be very quiet. She was so revered. After giving her a nice big hug, but not too hard for she was very frail, she would invite us to sit down. I noticed through the years she seemed to be fading away, but she always had a twinkle in her eyes and carried her Rosary intertwined between her fingers.

She had a box of chocolates on top of her safe and we got to choose a piece. Then ever so slowly, she reached down, opened her safe and pulled out a box of holy cards. They were wrapped in a white cloth and held together with a rubber band. How special it was to choose one. I always looked for a card that had an angel or two on it.

Some days she would be in that big 4-poster bed with the big fluffy pillows.

She had one of those large wooden rosaries on her pillow. She kept a smaller rosary by her side. It wouldn't surprise me if she said several rosaries each day.

She often asked about school, about our brothers and sisters, all in her true Gaelic accent.

Have you noticed that I have mentioned the Rosary several times? I would like to explain this beautiful prayer given to us by our Blessed Mother.

Pope John Paul II said, "To recite the Rosary is nothing other than to contemplate the face of Jesus with Mary". This method of prayer, a combination of vocal and contemplative prayer, has nourished the faith for generations of Christians. Pope John Paul II called on us Catholics and other Christians as well to pray the Rosary and enter "the school of Mary" who knew Jesus Christ so well as His Mother and who was His closest disciple.

The Rosary: Where did it come from? The beginnings of the Rosary go way back to the Christian practice of reciting the names of 150 Psalms from the Bible as a form of prayer. Those unable to recite the psalms started to recite the Our Father prayer using beads to count the prayers. By the middle ages, this custom was common in many countries. It became customary then to meditate on the life of Jesus from the Annunciation to Mary to His birth to His Ascension. The Hail Mary prayer is said on each bead of the Rosary 10 times as that mystery is contemplated.

In the year 1208, in France, the Albigensian Heresy was spreading in the Catholic Church. (This heresy denied the humanity of Christ.) St. Dominic who founded the Dominican Order was praying to God to help him with this problem. The Blessed Mother appeared to him with a "Rosary" in her hand and began to teach him how to pray. St Dominic then became its principle promoter. This devotion spread widely throughout the region and in time this heresy was wiped out. In 1566, Pope Pius V officially established the 15 mysteries of Our Lord's life. The Rosary was also called the "Psalter of the Blessed Virgin Mary". Pope St. Gregory XIII in 1573 set aside the first Sunday in October calling it the Feast of the Holy Rosary.

I would like to mention the various mysteries of the Rosary:

The Joyful Mysteries: the first joyful mystery is The Annunciation (Luke 1: 28) – Fruit of the Mystery: Humility, the second mystery is The Visitation of Mary to her cousin Elizabeth (Luke 1: 41-42) – Fruit of the Mystery: Love of Neighbor,

The third mystery is The Birth of Jesus (Luke 2:7) – Fruit of the Mystery is Poverty, the fourth mystery is The Presentation of Jesus in the Temple (Luke 2:22-23) – Fruit of the Mystery is Obedience, the fifth Joyful mystery is Finding the Child Jesus in the Temple (Luke 2:46) – Fruit of the Mystery is Joy in Finding Jesus.

The Sorrowful Mysteries: The first sorrowful mystery is The Agony in the Garden (Luke 22: 44-45) – Fruit of the Mystery is Sorrow for Sin, the second sorrowful mystery is The Scourging at the Pillar (John 19:1) – Fruit of the Mystery is Purity, the third sorrowful mystery is Crowning With Thorns (Mt: 27: 28-29) – Fruit of the Mystery is Courage, the fourth mystery is Carrying of the Cross (John 19: 17) – Fruit of the Mystery is Patience, the fifth sorrowful mystery is The Crucifixion (Luke 23:46) – Fruit of the Mystery is Perseverance.

The Glorious Mysteries: The first glorious mystery is The Resurrection (Mark 16:6) – Fruit of the Mystery is Faith, the second mystery is The Ascension (Mark 16:19) – Fruit of the Mystery is Hope, the third glorious mystery is Descent of the Holy Spirit (Acts 2:4) – Fruit of the Mystery is Love of God, the fourth mystery is The Assumption of Mary into Heaven (Judith 15: 9-10) – Fruit of the Mystery is Grace of a Happy Death, the fifth glorious mystery is The Coronation of Mary as Queen of Heaven and Earth (Rev: 12:1) – Fruit of the Mystery is Trust in Mary's Intercession.

Up to the present time, John Paul II added 5 more myster-

7

ies of Our Lord's life called The Luminous Mysteries: The first mystery is the Baptism of Jesus (Mt. 3: 16-17) – Fruit of the Mystery is Openness to the Holy Spirit, the second mystery is The Wedding Feast at Cana (John 2: 5-7) , the third mystery is Proclaiming the Kingdom (Mt. 10: 7-8) – Fruit of the Mystery is Repentance and Trust in God , the fourth mystery is the Transfiguration Luke 9: 29, 35) – Fruit of the Mystery is Desire For Holiness, and the fifth mystery is Institution of the Eucharist Luke 22: 19-20) – Fruit of the Mystery is Adoration .

All I can say about the Rosary is this. The Mother of God has given us this prayer in her effort to bring us closer to Jesus her Son. I don't think it matters much whether I like to pray it or not, I accept her invitation along with my prayer to her to help me learn how to pray in this way. By golly through the years she has done just that.

My cousin, Al Faber, Aunt Dorothy's son, sent me a couple of stories about Grandmother O'Brien:

On Saturday's the priests from Holy Trinity brought Holy Communion to grandma. My brother, Lucien, or I had the assignment of meeting the priest at the front door and with a lighted candle would lead him upstairs to her room. At one point grandma decided that the house needed painting and your father (Jim McCaffrey), who was working for the Pittsburgh Paint & Glass Co., volunteered to do the painting. He obtained a gas fired torch to heat the old paint to make it easier to chip off before applying the new paint. Disaster struck!!! The room where he started on the outside was grandma's room and it caught fire. The fire was extinguished without any real damage fortunately, but from then on grandma O'Brien had a real fear of fire.....Guess what? No more lighted candles for escort use.

Another story concerns her "featherbed" which was really made of down from ducks and geese----much softer than feathers. Anyway it was the softest bed I ever laid eyes on. Grandma took great pride in caring for her bed. After sleeping on it, there would be depressions wherever she had slept. She would painstakingly smooth out the "feather bed". Occasionally Lucien and

I would sneak into her room after she left to try out the softness, leaving it uneven. This bothered her and so one day she didn't leave but hid behind her closet and were two young men surprised when she suddenly appeared. Needless to say...no more playing on the bed!!!!

Grandmother O'Brien died September 26, 1948, at the age of 96. She is interred at the present Calvary Hill Cemetery. I remember her "wake". When you walked in the front door just to the left was the parlor. It was a long narrow room. Her open casket was located at the end of Aunt Dorothy's parlor for I think three days, perhaps less. She wore her black dress with a white lace collar and her rosary was entwined about her fingers. The room was rather dark with all that dark wood. I remember there were lace curtains on the windows. I was ten years old at the time, and I really just wanted this part to be over with. I knew she was at peace;

I would surely join her one day in God's Kingdom.

The memory of this sweet great grandmother Johannah Quinlan O'Brien will be forever etched in my heart. Right now a few tears are falling down my cheek. This is one of those precious present moments.

*M*y grandmother Marie Elizabeth was the third child and oldest daughter of Johannah and Patrick O'Brien. She was baptized on February 10,1886, at the Sacred Heart Cathedral in Dallas. She attended Ursuline Academy in Dallas. Grandmother met Homer Wilson and married him on October 3, 1906, at Sacred Heart Cathedral. Grandpa Wilson was a very gifted watch smith. People in Dallas brought their German clocks for him to repair. I took turns visiting him and grandmother in the summer.

Grandpa would take me to his little shop for the day. We took the streetcar down to his shop. How exciting it was to wind up all the clocks followed by the dusting of the counter tops. He would climb up on his stool, place his glasses on and attach a 3 tiered magnifying glass over one eye. I watched him a lot; he was steady as you go. To break the silence, every now and then, he would tell me another corny joke. He laughed and I did too, just to be courteous sometimes.

Grandma and Grandpa had three girls, my mom Frances Meron, Lillian Marie, and Dorothy Elaine. I'll tell more about these three girls later on.

Grandpa Wilson was born October 14, 1876 in Alvarado, Johnson County, Texas. He died on December 23, 1970, in Dallas. His father was James Madison Wilson, born September 1, 1846, in Tupelo County, Mississippi. He died in Terrell, Kaufman County Texas, on January 29, 1899, and is buried at the old Balch Cemetery in Alvarado. He married Lucy Caroline Richardson in 1867 in Johnson County. Apparently, James Madison had one of the only two saloons in Alvarado near a train station. One was called the First Chance Saloon, and the other the Last Chance Saloon.

My cousin, Rick Reed, provided this information on the Wilson Family: Thank you Rick.

James Madison divorced Lucy November 13, 1888. He remarried a lady by the name of M.J. Legg. James and Lucy Caroline had seven children:

1. Frank Wilson b. September 3, 1867 in Grandview, Johnson County, Texas and was married on October 23, 1887 to Mary Elizabeth Trent. He died on March 12, 1938, and is buried at the Rosemead Cemetery, McClennan County, Waco, Texas.
2. Gertrude Wilson b. 1888 in Johnson County, to Sherrod William Seaman. She died on May 17, 1945 in Palo Pinto County, Mineral Wells, Texas.
3. Lillian Wilson b. February 16, 1872 in Alvarado, Texas, and married December 25, 1887, in Johnson County, to Sidney Thomas Smith. She died on August 10, 1963 in Decatur, Dekalb County, and is buried in the Decatur Cemetery.
4. Coreen A. Wilson b. December 24, 1874, in Alvarado, Texas, and married in 1897 to Walter Collins (a lawyer). She died August 7, 1952, in Fort Worth, and is buried in the Ridge Park Cemetery in Hillsboro, Texas.
5. Homer T. Wilson (my grandfather) b. October 14, 1876, in Alvarado, Texas and married October 3, 1906 to Mary Elizabeth O'Brien. He died December 23, 1970.
6. Louis Wilson b. September 17, 1882, in Alvarado, Texas and married in 1910 to Claudine Rotan in Dallas, Texas. He died on October 1, 1971 in Dallas, and is buried at the Oak Grove Memorial Park in Dallas. He was a lawyer.
7. Ruby Adran Wilson b. November 2, 1883, in Alvarado, Texas. She was blind from birth or shortly after. She never married and died on December 4, 1940 in Fort Worth, Texas. She is buried next to her mother Lucy Caroline Wilson in Alvarado, Texas, at the Glenwood Cemetery.

Frank was a saloon keeper like his father. Gertrude's husband Sherrod was a blacksmith. Lillian's husband Sidney, died in Waco, and was a liquor dealer.

Coreen remarried C.C. Farmer after her husband Walter

died. She divorced soon after. Louis was a lawyer in Dallas and there is a picture of him at the Dallas Bar Association. Ruby was a gifted musician and went to school for music. She played until she died.

Grandpa and Grandma Wilson lived at 1421 Bennett Avenue, Dallas, Texas, 75208, just off Fitzhugh. They owned a two story frame house divided into four apartments. I loved visiting them. The furniture was dark mahogany. Grandma's front parlor was done up in dark blue velvet cushions with lace curtains. I loved sitting in this quiet spot browsing through the books and albums. Grandpa loved baseball. On the weekend he would be sitting next to his radio with that fan-like dial. He used a straight razor to shave with. I always wondered what kind of soap he used to lather up with that brush. I have his shaving cup. For several years he would take me on the streetcar to Fair Park for the Ice Capades in October during the State Fair. We celebrated our October birthdays together. Sonja Heine was the most graceful skater with her white plumed costumes. I was taking ice skating lessons myself, and I remember I would think of her as I glided around the ice with my arms out just so.

Grandpa had this little coin purse in his pocket. He kept a row of nickels and dimes in each section. Depending on our age, he would click open one section and we got to pick out a coin. Then in his coat pocket were hard candies and we got to reach in for one. I remember that he would put his index finger inside of his cheek and make that popping sound and then chuckle. He wore those high top laced, black shoes with white socks. He always dressed in his suit and tie.

Now I am happy to tell you about my Grandmother Wilson. At one time Grandma owned and operated a millinery store at 301 S. Ervay. I have a picture of the shop. She was always cheerful, always there for us. She too, like her mother Johannah, prayed her rosary every day. How she loved the Blessed Mother. She was always so considerate of others. Her faith was strong. She baked a certain white coconut cake for Easter. It was scrumptious! She used ½ lb. of butter and ½ cup of Wesson Oil.

She would talk on that long-necked phone to my mom, to Aunt Lillian, and to Aunt Dorothy frequently. Her daily routine was simple. During my summer visit, we would walk around the corner to that small grocery store to get food for a day or two. The grocery store had a creaking wooden floor. I thought it was so quaint. Grandma bought Del Monte vegetables, and a certain kind of bread. Her meals were always nourishing. She didn't believe in snacking between meals. Later on, when she would come over and look after us while Mom was at the hospital having another baby, she always stayed back in the kitchen. One day Angela and I made our phone ring and while one of us told Grandma it was for her, the other one would sneak back into the kitchen to grab a little snack. For lunch she always prepared a small piece of meat, a hot vegetable, and two leaves of lettuce, two slices of tomatoes topped with a dollop of mayo. She and Grandpa had a bowl of cereal for supper.

It was like a tradition that I would go down the street to Ross Avenue and get a permanent during my yearly summer sojourn to Grandma's house. In those days, they used those long, heavy, hot curlers hanging down. They sat there, heavy on my head. Good grief, I thought, why didn't God give me some natural curl? Then I had to deal with the frizzes for awhile until those curls calmed down.

Occasionally, Grandma would buy my Christmas or Easter dress, along with the dress came a spanking new pair of socks, underwear, and black, patent leather Mary Jane shoes. That dress was my "Sunday go to meeting dress" for as long as it fit and then it was passed down to the next sister.

On Sunday, Grandma and I would walk up to Ross Avenue and take the bus to Sacred Heart Cathedral for Holy Mass. This beautiful, red brick structure with the large stained glass windows of the Saints is a land mark even today. The pews were made of dark wood that creaked when you knelt down. Oh, I thought, this is really an ancient house of God. Grandma was baptized there on February 10, 1886. My mother, Frances, was baptized, confirmed, and married in this same cathedral. (More about Mom later)

I noticed that Grandpa never went to Church with us. Grandma would say, "He is a good man and God loves him." At night, when I said my prayers, I would ask God not to forget my Grandpa and of course He didn't.

Now I will interject the story of my Grandfather's baptism the night before he went to Heaven. It was the Christmas season of 1970. Grandpa was 94 at the time. My mom had brought my grandparents to her house on Gooding Drive. She fixed up a nice room for them. She left the house to do some shopping. Grandpa and Grandma were resting when the phone rang. It was out in the den. Grandpa got up, shuffled down the hall. He had to step down several steps to answer the phone and he fell, breaking his hip. He called out to Grandma and alarmed, she rose up quickly and fell, having a mild stroke to boot. Meanwhile, my sister dropped by to visit and discovered the situation. Sure enough, Grandpa had broken his hip and was transported to St.Paul's Hospital. Grandma was also transported later on because she also sustained a broken hip. Grandpa's cardiac status was good, so his hip was fixed. Grandma got pneumonia and left this world for Heaven on December 19, 1970, at the age of 85.

GRANDPA HOMER T. AND GRANDMA MARIE O'BRIEN WILSON

Grandpa was ready to be discharged. Mom had arranged a walker and hospital bed for him. Well, the day before he was to be released, Grandpa called the Sister and asked for baptism. He told her there was no use in him sticking around. He fell asleep that night and drifted right up to Heaven. How beautiful, to leave this world like that. It was December 23, 1970.

Grandpa and Grandma Wilson brought a lot of fun and joy into my life. I always looked forward to their visits and my visits to their home. They didn't talk a lot about their growing up and that is why I am writing my recollections of them. I want my children and grandchildren to know about this grandmother's family.

THE O'BRIENS
MARIE – DENNIS – DOROTHY – MONK – ELLA – FRANK

I'd like to mention some of my Grandmother Wilson's brothers and sisters since we saw them through the years. Patrick and Johannah had ten children:

1. William Patrick b. December 28, 1881, died April 20, 1964. Uncle Will operated the family farm at Hutchins until 1951. He was a gentle person and could remember facts. He was always seated in the front parlor when he visited. He had those bushy O'Brien eyebrows.

2. David Michael, Uncle Dave, b. January 9, 1884, died March 24, 1961. He studied engineering at Dallas University from 1915-1917 and had a plumbing business.

3. Marie Elizabeth (my Grandmother) born December 1, 1885 and died December 21, 1970. I have written previously concerning her.

4. Ellen Josephine, Aunt Ella, born September 12, 1887, died December 23, 1981. She graduated from Ursuline Academy and married Julius Carl Vogel on April 3, 1910. We would drop by every now and then to visit her family, Mary Beth, who married Ed Lindeman. They have one daughter, Mariellin. Father Carl, ordained a Catholic priest on May 27, 1950. (Fr. Carl passed away August 2008 – God rest his soul.) Michael Donald married our next door neighbor, Mary Ann Triece. They have six children. Patricia Jane married James A. Moran and they have four children.

5. Reginald Joseph (Uncle Monk), was born August 8, 13, 1890, and died August 8, 1964. He remained single and was paymaster at Dallas Power and light. He was known for his generosity. He was the shortest of my uncles.

6. Francis Charles (Uncle Frank) was born September 9, 24, 1892 and died January 5, 1974. He also remained single and had those bushy eyebrows. He practiced law in Dallas and became a Judge in Dallas in 1935. A couple of my brothers had to go before him in court on traffic violations. One brother said, "Hello, Uncle Frank," but that didn't lessen the situation one bit. There is a

story about Uncle Frank and his younger brother, Uncle Dennis. In 1910, the Halley Comet was expected to be near the earth in order to be seen. On May 19, Frank and Dennis caught a crow and tied a wire to its tail with a ball of rags at the end of the wire. They soaked the rags in kerosene, lit them, and turned the crow loose. The next day in the Dallas Morning News there was a report that many people had personally seen Halley's Comet north of Dallas on the night of May 19.

Many years later, in late 1973, Charles and I were visiting my mom on Gooding Drive in Dallas. Our daughter Colleen was just a baby and Kirk was two. Aunt Dorothy called and asked if we could drive her and Uncle Frank out to the farm in Louisville, Texas, where they had grown up. Uncle Frank was quite ill at the time. We took pictures of this venture. The farm and house are still there. Then we drove to a certain spot off of Lake Dallas, where Uncle Frank said they played as kids. He walked out to the bank and stood awhile absorbed in his memories. He died shortly after that.

Father Carl relates that he stopped by in December, 1973, to visit Uncle Frank. Frank was reading his Bible and Father Carl asked him why. Uncle Frank said, "I'm cramming for my final."

7. Christopher Alphonso was Uncle Frank's twin and died three days after his birth on September 27, 1892.

8. Jeanette Margarite, born December 1, 1894, and died December 21, 1936, at the age of 32. She was single. I never knew her.

9. Justin Dennis, our beloved Uncle Dennis, was born October 5, 1866, and died May 6, 1964. Uncle Dennis became a general practitioner in Medicine. He delivered many of my mother's babies. He told the nurses not to wake my mother during the night, she needed the rest. We would go to downtown Dallas to his office in the Medical Arts Building to get a checkup for one reason or other. He was always kind to us.

Uncle Dennis married Alice Mary Hickey on January 13, 1930. They had two children, Alice Carol who married Robert Macauly, and they have four children. Also, Neil Justin, who married Patricia Margaret Brown, and they had four children. Neil is my cousin who wrote "A Brief History of The O'Brien Clan."

10. Dorothy Clara O'Brien was born March 5, 1899, and died February 4, 1995. She was the youngest child of Patrick and Johannah. She also graduated from Ursuline Academy in 1917. She married Uncle Albert Anthony Faber. They had three children, Albert Anthony Jr., Dorothy Anne, and Lucien Patrick.

Al Faber and Clara have nine children; Beverly Ann, Susan Patricia, Anthony, Linda Ruth, Glenda Edward, Stephen Russell, Gordon Christopher, Charles August, and Daniel Robert. Alan has passed away.

Dorothy Ann was born and died on June 29, 1935. The Mass of the Angels was said for her and my sister, Mary Elise McCaffrey, who died on June 28 at the age of 18 months.

Lucien Patrick married Kathleen Margaret McCambridge. They have five children: Scott Patrick, Laura Paige, Kimberly Jo, Leslie Michelle, and Lucien Todd. Lucien Patrick , nicknamed Duke, has passed away.

Through the years Aunt Dorothy and Uncle Albert would drop off a bushel basket of fruit at Christmas. Taped to the top were little envelopes with money inside for each of us. The older you got, the more money. Boy, I was wishing to grow up real fast. What a joy!

Before Aunt Dorothy moved into Grandmother O'Brien's house on Gilbert she lived way out in the country off NW highway. JoAnne, Angela, Eileen and I loved playing on her swing set. She always had cold drinks iced down.

When I was about nine, I went several summers to Aunt Dorothy's house to help her with various chores. The most enjoyable one was serving meals to Grandmother O'Brien. I would peak into her room to see how things were going, and many times she would be in prayer.

How we all loved Aunt Dorothy. On a visit to my Mom's she was in St.Paul's Hospital, very ill with cancer. I drove Mom over to see her one morning. She was very weak. She had just completed her morning bath and looked real pretty in her pink nightgown. She still had that lovely smile. The over bed table was up in front of her with the little mirror up too. She took out her Mary Kay cosmetics, lined them up and applied the moisturizer first, ever so slowly. Then she rested followed by the day radiance foundation. Then she rested again. Next was the eye shadow and blush. Then she rested again. All of this took about thirty minutes. Later, she applied the finishing touch, pst pst... her cologne! I just sat there amazed. I was thinking this was an external way of showing her self esteem. She died a few days later.

I don't want to forget my Mom's sister, Aunt Lillian. She would drop by and visit us and we would share our life with her. She was like a "big sister" to us. She was a good listener and always kind.

MOM AND AUNT LILLIAN

Aunt Lillian Marie was born on June 14, 1916, in Dallas. By the way, she is 91 today but has since passed away. She graduated from Ursuline Academy in 1934. She received her A.R.T. Degree as a Medical Record Librarian. She worked many years at St.

Paul's Hospital. She married Calvin Gordon Reed on March 19, 1946. She and Calvin have three boys, Richard (Ricky) Gordon, married to Maria Guadalupe Robleda-Gonzales de Castilla and they have three children, Richard, Angela Francesca married to Hugh Lamar Stone, and Cecilia Maria married to Michael Frances Hagan and they have a child Lilliana Hagan. Aunt Lillian's second child is Ronald Patrick married to Lana Benge and they have three children Kelly Gene, Lisa Marie married to Frederick Marsh . Lisa and Fred have two children, Kristian and Alexis. Ron's third child is Shawn with two children Dylan and Noah. Aunt Lillian's third child is Tim.

I never knew my mother's third sister, Aunt Dorothy Elaine. She was born on December 12, 1922. She loved music and was of a gentle nature, so they say. She died at age 24, November 22, 1937 of burns received when her dress caught fire while dressing for church. My Dad ran from an apartment across the hall, and beat out the flames.

We shared many happy days with the Wilsons!

THE MCCAFFREYS

*N*ow, I would like to proceed to my Dad's side of the family, the McCaffreys. My cousins Kevin and John Pat compiled information on "The McCaffreys in America."

Up front, I want to list the genealogical line of John Alden (who came over on the Mayflower in 1620) from the Mullins, Pabodie and Simmons families, to the great, great, grand children of Israel Brownell, one of whom was Jennie Minerva Brownell, who married my great grandfather, Charles John McCaffrey. If you will bear with me, I will follow the families to show I am a distant relative of John Alden. Hang on there's more… John Alden married Priscilla Mullins in 1621. Their daughter, Elizabeth Alden, married William Pabodie in 1644. William and Elizabeth had a daughter, Mercy, in 1649, who married John Simmons in 1669. Mercy and John had a son, William, who married Abigail Church in 1696. William and Abigail had a son, John, in 1704. John Simmons married Comfort Shaw in 1728. They had a daughter, Rachel, in 1751, who married Israel Brownell. Rachel and Israel had a son, Frederick, in 1794, who married Ann Dawley in 1818. He and Ann had a son, Elijah Hanchett, in 1828. Elijah Brownell married Sarah Ann Warman in 1859. He and Sarah had a daughter, Jennie Minerva, who married my great grandfather Charles John McCaffrey.

Now I find this rather interesting. The McCaffreys came from Northern Ireland, in County Fermanaugh, situated on the South Western border of the Northern Province of Ulster. Fermanaugh is distinctive in that it is bisected by the Loughs or Lake Ernes. Enniskillen is the County seat. Today, the county is known for its ancient monuments and scenic vistas. The actual McCaffrey homeland is at Ballymacafry, which lies in the Clougher valley, NE of Enniskillen. The green hills and blue waters have enticed visitors for years. Fermanaugh is the home of the Belick china makers.

The McCaffrey or McCaffery family originated with the

first kings of the northern Irish county of Fermanaugh. The first McCaffery was the son of Donn Mor Maguire, ancestor of all the Maguire kings of Fermanaugh. Gafraidh in the Gaelic means Godfrey, hence the clan name Mc (son of) Caffery, means son of Godfrey. The first McCafferys took hold of their parcel of SE Fermanaugh in 1302, the year King Don Mor died. To this day you will find all kinds of McCafferys, McCaffreys in county Fermanaugh.

The McCaffreys were a tight knit clan. They acted as a group. In 1533, Redmond Maguire insulted the wife of Cormac Mac Gafraidg. The annals tell us that the clan Mac Gafraidg refused to let the insult pass and hunted down and slew Redmond.

I want to mention the Penal Laws. The victorious English, commenced to demand loyalty to the crown from all Irish by way of the Penal Laws in the early 18th century. The purpose of the laws, according to one Professor Lecky, was "to make them poor and keep them poor." Native Irish Catholics were subject to the following laws in their own country by the Protestant majority:

They could not receive an education, enter a profession, hold public office, engage in trade, live within five miles of a corporation (Protestant) town, vote, keep or bear arms, buy life insurance, inherit anything from a Protestant, or educate a child. In an effort to divorce people from their faith, the Protestants legislated that Catholics had to attend Protestant worship. Catholic clergy were banned in the entire country after a set date. Catholic clergy found after that date would be banished. If they returned, the state would "draw, quarter, and then hang the papist criminal."

To insure that Catholics could never amass wealth the following prohibitions were installed: Catholics could not purchase land, lease land, inherit land, accept a mortgage on land as security for a loan, own a horse worth more than five pounds, rent land worth more than thirty shillings a year, or reap profit from land worth more than one third of his rent. If any Catholic was found to have wealth in excess of one third of his rent, the "finder" would reap the excess as personal gain.

The Catholic family was also a target. Wives who were unfaithful could convert to Protestantism and expect an annuity from the cuckolded husband. If a child converted, he/she would be the sole beneficiary of the family's inheritance, regardless of other or older children.

This English-Scottish effort to destroy the Irish Catholic identity again failed to extinguish the Irish spirit. The cumulative effect of the laws was to drive a wedge permanently between English and Irish people. Although there was widespread flouting of the laws, sometimes with dire consequences, most of these acts remained the law of the land for the entire 18th century. The laws were maintained by an Irish Parliament in Dublin which represented the Protestant landlord class.

The Irish refused to submit to many of these English laws. They resorted to hedge schools and midnight masses to clandestinely keep the faith alive. The Penal Laws were eventually repealed, many through the efforts of Daniel O'Connell (the Liberator). He managed to get Catholics to vote, then was the first Catholic to win a seat in Parliament from County Clare. This breakthrough led to a reassessment of Irish Law and a new attitude towards Catholics in Ireland and England.

I would be remiss if I didn't mention the potato famine which lasted from 1845 through1847. Several million people left the country including my relatives the O'Brien's, the Quinlans and McCaffreys, all of whom settled in America. You see, the potato was the most important staple of the Irish worker.

So, my dad, Jim McCaffrey's family, hailed from a clan in the village of Enniskillen, on Locherne in the county of Fermanaugh, Ireland. My great, great Grandfather John was the eldest son of Patrick McCaffrey and Susan Harris. He was born in 1813, and came to America, where he sent for his two sisters and a brother. John is buried in Dayton, Ohio. His wife, Susan, born in 1832, is buried in Springfield, Ohio.

GREAT GRANDFATHER CHARLES
JOHN MCCAFFREY

GREAT GRANDMOTHER JENNIE
MINERVA BROWNELL MCCAFFREY

John had two children, Charles John, born May 18, 1853, who married Jennie Brownell, born in 1863. They had six children; John Horace, 1885(my grandfather), we called him Pop. Other children were, Charlie, Harry, Bernice and Katherine. My great, great grandfather, Jennie Brownell's dad, Elijah, was born June 20, 1828, in Salisbury Township, Herkimer County, New York. He died July 7, 1911, at 160 Maple Street, Dayton. Montgomery County, Ohio. He is buried in Woodland Cemetery, Dayton, Ohio.

Jennie Minerva Brownell McCaffrey's mother was Sarah Ann Warman of Dayton, Ohio, born September 1, 1842 in Springville, Harmony Township, and Warren County, New Jersey. She died on Thursday, October 16, 1902, at 160 Maple Street in Dayton. She is buried in Woodland Cemetery in Dayton. She was the daughter of Caleb and Margaret (Rush) Warman.

Jennie Brownell had ten brothers and sisters, all born in Ohio; Pheba Emma, Minnie Ann, who married Louis Frevert, Frederick Charles, who married May Moore McIntire, Addison

Lincoln, who married Alma Smith, Clara Berentha, who married Dr. William Holden, Margaret Rush, who died at childbirth and is buried on the Brownell farm in Richland Township, Logan County, Ohio, Sadie Olivia, who married Dr.Harrie Guy, Elijah Elsworth, who married May Etta Leiter, Nellie Frances, who married James Courtland Campbell, and Dolly Eugenia, who married Herbert Lee Kanmachtler. Whew! Now you can take a breath.

I would like to include the account of the tragic death of Thomas Brownell in 1664 to show the wording and way of expression. Thomas was a distant relative of my great grandmother Jennie Minerva Brownell McCaffrey. The spelling of the words is very interesting.

TRAGIC DEATH OF THOMAS BROWNELL
Testimony of Daniel Lawton at the inquest of
Thomas Brownell

The Testimony of Daniell Layton aged about twenty one years or thereabouts being according to law upon oath engaged testifyeth in the afternoon Mr. Thomas Brownell being at the deponants fathers house, Mr. Brownell asked the deponent whither he would ride towards Portsmouth Town along with him, the deponent answered he would. Soe they both ride together, and when they were come down the hill at the head of William Wodels grownd, Mr. Brownell put his horse on a gallop afore the deponent, whereupon this deponent also put on his horse and presently outrun Mr. Brownelland got afore him, and soe continued on his gallop some distance of wayafore he looktback but at length looking back to see where Mr. Brownell was he sped his horse running alone out of the way into the swamp, whereupon this deponent forth with, not mistrusting eminent danger to the man ran and turned the horse and brought him into the way where presently he saw Mr. Brownell lying on the ground, and the deponent called but none answering he let the horse goe and went up to him and took him by the arms, whereby and also by the effusion of very much blood from him

25

on the ground he perceived the sayd Mr. Brownell was dead. This deponent doth testify the above written

Before us the 25th of September 1664

William Baulston, Asst

John Sanford, Asst

These to the coroner Mr. William Baulston Assistant – Wee of the inquest apoyented and ingaged to sitt on the body or corps of Thomas Brownell of Portsmouth: who was found dead on the high way against the upper end of the land of William Wodell yesterday being the 24th of this instant month.

This is our return judgement and sence thereon, we find by evident signs and apeerances, as a very great effusion of blood, and the raines of his bridle being broken and lying neer by him, as also an apparent signs of a stroke on a tree neereto where he lay and some blood and hair sticking on the sayd throwne or dashed against the sayd tree, and his skull broke and to our understanding his brains came out. This finding was the cause of his death.

Signed with the full agreement and consent of the rest of the jury the 25th Sept 1664.

Samuell Willbure, Forman

The following is the will of Thomas Brownell (9-16-1665) on my great Grandmother Jennie Brownell's side.

WILL OF THOMAS BROWNELL
(Made by the Town Council of Portsmouth, Rhode Island)
Dated September the 16th Ano Dom 1665 Portsmouth, Rhode Island Scrap-book

Whereas by the wonderful provedence of almighty god Thomas Brownell of the town of Portsmouth within the Collony of Rhode Island and providence plantations in New England in America Deceased on the 24th day of September last past (1664) And not having a will how and to whom his Estate should be divided. Therefore and in pursuance of that power by the law of this Collony to us Commited and the Reall Setiment of the

Estate of the Sayd deceased Thomas Brownell Wee the Counsell of the Towne of Portsmouth with the free and vollentary Consent of Ann Brownell Widow to the Sayd deceased Thomas Brownell upon (worn) and deliberate Consideration do hereby Declare as the will of the deceased that wee do hereby apoynte and impower the Sayd Ann Brownell whole and Sole Exequetrix to the estate of her deceased Husband Thomas Brownell to Receive and pay all debts to (worn) all Bargains and Covenants to be performed and Especaly with Mr. William Brenton concerning the Exchanging of Lands, to perform and pay and make good all the several Legasies to her severall children as hereafter is Exprest Wee doe therefore agree and order that the Sayd Ann Brownell is to have the use Benefitt and profit of all the housing and Lands of the Sayd Deceased Thomas Brownell untill the time of the marridge of her Eldist sonn George or till he come to the age of one and twenty years, at Either of which time the Sayd George Brownell shall have and possess the one half of the land it being at the apoyntment of the Exequetrix which half is (worn) possession of the sayd Ann untill the time of her death at which time all the Lands and housing aforesaid Shall Return unto the Sayd George Brownell Eldist sonn to the deceased Thomas Brownell or to his heirs if he have any, if not then the Land and Housing shall go to the next Eldist sonn of the deceased Thomas Brownell that Shall then be living or to his lawful heirs only if the Sayd Exequetrix should Decease before the time of the performance of the Several Legacies then the Sayd George Brownell or who shall posses the Lands shall pay and perform the Severall Legacies at the time hereafter Specified, that shall then be unpayed. And wee doe order that Robert Brownell second sonn to the deceased Shall have the some of Twenty pounds which Shall be payd to him at the age of one and twenty years, and to William Brownell the third sonn wee order the some of Twenty pounds to be payed him at the age of one and Twenty (worn) the some ten shillings to be payd to Mary Hazard Eldist daughter to the Sayd deceased Thomas Brownell and to be forthwith payd unto her: and wee doe order that Sarah ffreeborn the second daughter Shall have the Some of tenn Shillings forthwith payd unto her and to Martha Brownell the third daughter wee doe order the some of Twenty pounds to be payd to her at the day of her marriage: and wee doe order that Ann Brownell the fourth daughter shall have the some of Twenty pounds payd unto her at the day of marridge: And we agree and order that Susanah Brownell the ffifth daughter shall have the Some of Twenty pounds payd unto her at the day of her marridge: And we agree and order that if any of the aforenamed Robert, William, Thomas, Martha, Ann, Susanah if either shall Die before the payment of their Legacie or without heirs then the Legacies of the deceased shall be divided amongst those of the fore named six that Shall then be living and in Ratifygation and Confirmation of the Sayd

Act order and agreement wee have hereunto putt our hands the day and yeare aforesaid.

WILLIAM BAULSTON	SAMUEL WILBUR
Asistant	Asistant
JOHN ALBROJOHN	BRIGSJOHN SANFORD
(his L mark)	

Shall we continue the McCaffrey saga? Great, great Grandfather John, as reported by my dad's brother, Uncle John, grew rich in the nursery business. He spoke several languages, was an artist and musician. He could read Greek and Latin. And he was liked by everyone.

This story is about a young Irish immigrant who became a wealthy entrepreneur, who at the age of 39 married a young woman of twenty, Susan Harris. At this time of the Civil War he was a widower with two small children, Charles John and Susan Catherine. John at this time, owned 500 acres of prime farm and forest land in Wells County, Indiana, as well as property in Springfield, Ohio. He died on November 11, 1881 in Dayton, Ohio. Susan died on February 26, 1855. I am proud to be the great, great granddaughter of John and Susan McCaffrey.

My great, great grandfather John, immigrated to America around 1835, ten years before the potato famine. His father, Patrick, my great, great, great grandfather came to America sometime between 1846 and 1853. Remember the potato famine took place in 1845-1846. Patrick married Susan Harones and they had six children; Bridget (Biddy),born in 1809, Catherine, born in1812 and married Edwin McCartin, John born in 1813, who married Susan Harris, born in 1823, a twin to John by the name of James, born in 1813, and married Bessie Reid, Mary, who remained in Ireland, and Charles who died young.

Charles John McCaffrey and Jennie Brownell had six children; John, born in 1883, Horace, born in 1885 (my grandfather) who married Mary Lucinda Klepfer, born in 1884, then married Clara Braun, born in 1889, Charlie, born in 1888, Harry, born in 1890, Bernice born in 1893, and Katherine.

I have just received more information about my grandmother Mary Lucinda Klepfer from my cousin Kevin McCaffrey, Uncle Nute's son:

Mary Lucinda Klepfer was the fourth child of six of John H. Klepfer and May West Klepfer. She was born 6-30-1884 in Bradford, Pa. in McKean County. Her nickname was Molly. She was named after her maternal grandmother, Mary Jane Litz. Her middle name, Lucinda, came from her paternal grandmother Lucinda Keck.

Both the Klepfer and West families had long settled in Pennsylvania. John's father, who would be my great, great grandfather, Reuben Klepfer, was a wagon maker. (See 1870 U.S. census, Pa, Clarion County, pg 27 line 16, dated 6-16-1870.) May's father, who would be my other great, great grandfather, James Harvey West, was a shoemaker and was also born in Pa. (See 1880 U.S. census, Pa, McKean County, Pg 96, line 10, dated 6-28-1880.),

According to family stories:

John Klepfer joined a railroad company. He may have been assigned to work in McKean County. He married May West 8-5-1878. Their first daughter Vira Maud was born 8-8-1879. James

29

Reuben came next on 5-11-1880 where they lived at Sawyer City, McKean County, Pa.

Meanwhile, in 1880 John's parents were living in Venaugo County and May's parents were living in nearby McKean County.

On 2-14-1882, the third born of John and May joined the family, Metta Zoe. Then along came Mary Lucinda (my grandmother). Her sister Vera died soon after her birth.

In the spring of 1885, the family moved west to Nebraska.

Nebraska was described as follows:

Permanent settlement in Nebraska was forbidden until 1854 because the region was maintained as Indian country. Finally the Kansas-Nebraska Act was passed by Congress and created two new territories. Inhabitants were allowed to settle and to decide if they wanted slavery. Early explorers gave reports of it being a giant desert unfit for farming. The Homestead Act of 1862 provided free land to settlers. The prospect of free land and the Union Pacific Railroad starting through Nebraska in 1865 encouraged people to move into the area. In 1867 Nebraska became a State.

The western section was native grassland and was good for livestock. People who settled in this area built sod houses because there was little timber. Mary Lucinda mentioned that once she lived in a house with dirt floors and that one night she had to ride bareback on horse to get a doctor.

In 1874 the grasshopper invasion drove many settlers back east. In 1880-1881, whole herds of cattle perished in the blizzard and sleet storms. In 1890 a drought condition began that lasted 11 years. By 1891 thousands of farm families headed east.

While living in Red Willow County, located on the southwest border of Nebraska, May Klepfer had her fifth child, Kittie Clementine, born 8-10-1886. Kittie later related to her children that indeed she lived in a sod house in Nebraska.

Sod was a blessing to the pioneers. With no trees or stones in sight to build their houses from, the very earth they walked on was a perfect solution. The sod was cheap, easily accessible, and provided excellent insulation. To cut the sod, settlers used a tool called a cutting plow, which had a set of adjustable rods to cut the sod into rows about three to six inches thick and a foot wide. The rows were then cut into bricks. The sod was laid grass side down, like bricks, in side by side rows. Three rows of sod would make a thick wall that could support the weight of the house. Seams between the sod bricks were staggered to keep the walls as tight as possible. Every third or fourth layer of sod was laid crosswise to bind the stacks together. The women helped too. They would shave the inside and outside walls with a sharp spade. Housekeeping and cooking were difficult in a sod house. Often families covered the walls with muslim or whitewash to try and keep the dirt out of the living and cooking areas. Bugs, mice, snakes and dirt falling from the ceiling was frustrating. Are you wondering how to heat such a structure? Because wood was sparse and coal was expensive, buffalo and cowdroppings, or "chips", were used for fuel. No problem with the smell, the family would rather be warm. Here's how to collect the chips. Each picker would tie a rope to the handle of an old washtub and pull it around the grass and thus pick up all the chips they could find.

Kittie related also that the family returned to Bowling Green, Ohio around 1890-1891. Grandmother Mary Lucinda was 6 or 7 at this time. Kitty did not know the reason for this move but it was an upsetting experience.

It is assumed that Mary Lucinda's father, John, stayed behind with the railroad co.

On Feb 15, 1891, Jay West Klepfer was born, the sixth child of May & John. Great Grandmother May unfortunately died 13 days later at the age of 30. Jay West died in August of the same year.

Mary Lucinda's father, John, did return to Ohio and he purchased eight cemetery lots for his family in Bowling Green, Ohio. John made what must have been a difficult and painful decision to leave his children with May's parents. Life was harsh enough in the wilderness and who would look after his children? So it is presumed that John returned to Nebraska and supported his family from a distance. It is believed that he had a job of some importance that he could not leave. He had intentions of returning to Ohio to be buried with his wife and children but the last place he was heard from was Red Willow, Nebraska.

So, James Reuben, 11, Metta Zoe 9, and Mary Lucinda 7, went to live with their grandparents, James & Mary West in Prairie Depot, Ohio. Kittie Clementine, 5, went to live with her Aunt Kittie Gibson West and her husband Ellis Wilson in Findlay, Ohio.

It is noted that the Cemetery Records Department, city of Bowling Green, indicates that lot # 526 in the circle section (at Oak Grove Cemetery) was purchased by John Klepfer on 2-28-1891.

At the age of 15, Mary Lucinda was in school in Freeport Village (Prairie Village), Montgomery Township, Wood County Ohio.

Mary Lucinda's maternal grandfather, James Harvey West was 61 around 1899, in poor health and died later that year 7 days before Christmas. This means he was born around 1838.

After her grandfather James West died, Mary Lucinda moved on to Montpelier, Indiana, a boom town at the turn of the century. Her uncle, Lewis Litz West, and his wife, Arminta, took her in. Lewis was an oil well contractor.

Now here we are getting close to the meeting of my paternal grandmother Mary Lucinda to my grandfather Horace McCaffrey who was living with his parents, Charles John and Jennie Minerva Brownell McCaffrey.

Mary Lucinda worked as a telephone operator and met Horace who was a paint salesman for Patton Paint Co in Montpelier. On Feb. 27, 1904, Horace, age 19, married Mary Lucinda Klepfer, age 20. Rev. C.W. Brown officiated at this Sacrament of matrimony. (See the Marriage Certificate No.247, Book "F", Blackford County Circuit Court, Indiana.)

Their first born was Uncle John who came into this world July

7, 1905. I'll just mention some stories about him. He became quite an artisan in stain glass window design. He would travel around the country visiting Churches to do some repair work on their windows. He was General Patton's barber in Africa. He battled Alcoholism throughout his life. He would drop in to visit us from time to time. He spent some time at the Trappist Monastery in Conyers, Ga. working as a handy man. My Dad used to go there for his annual retreat at Easter. I presume Dad got him this job. I'm not sure where he died but I was told he was alone.

GRANDFATHER HORACE (POP) AND MARY LUCINDA KLEPFER MCCAFFREY

Pop and Grandmother Mary Lucinda headed to south Texas. Pop sold hardware and travelled all over Texas. For a short time they lived in Corsicana, Tx. where Aunt Ruth Clare was born 2-7-1907. Aunt Ruth told of her birth as related by her mother as follows:

While Pop was on another selling trip, Mary Lucinda and her 19 month John were left in a room above the town saloon. She was near term with Ruth Clare. They were very poor. At night Mary Lucinda would go downstairs into the saloon and look for some food. A midwife helped with the birth. All through the delivery the same song kept playing over and over from below in the saloon.

Moving along my Dad James Horace was born 10-8-1909 in Waco, Texas. In the 1910 U.S. Census the family was reported living in Dallas, Tx. at 219 Grand Ave. (See 1910 U.S. census, Texas, Dallas County, 7th ward, Vol. 35, ED 55, Sheet 14, line 30.) Pop was listed as a hardware salesman, age 25, and Mary Lucinda, also 25 was keeping house. Uncle John was 5, Ruth was 3 and my Dad, Jim, was 6 months. Two more children were born while living in Dallas, Charles Joseph, Uncle C.J., born 8-7-1914, and Horace Jr, Uncle Nute, born 2-10-1916.

Around 1921 Mary Lucinda and pop moved up to Milwaukee,Wis. Pop was working for Pittsburgh Plate Glass Co. as a salesman. (By the way my Dad worked for this same co after he married Mom.) They moved there in a touring car and camped out on the shore of Lake Michigan until Pop could find suitable housing. In 1938 Pop was living at 5135 W Roosevelt Dr, Milwaukee, Wis.

Grandmother Mary Lucinda suffered from Diabetes. She had what we call brittle Diabetes and was on insulin therapy. She lost some toes from this disease.

Mary Lucinda was often left with the children while Pop travelled on business. She was loved and admired by her husband and children. She would cut and sell her hair to bring in extra money. While living in Milwaukee, she and Pop financially adopted two boys, Charles Albrecht and Danny Bartz.

As her children grew old enough, Mary would accompany Pop on a business trip. It was on March 27, 1938, at the age of 54, that she died in her sleep of a coronary thrombosis in a hotel in Omaha, Neb. She was buried at Holy Cross Cemetery 3-30-1938.

It has been a real pleasure to script this information about my grandmother Mary Lucinda Klepfer McCaffrey. I look forward to our meeting in the hereafter.

To summarize my grandfather Horace (Pop) and Mary Lucinda Klepfer had five children; John, born 7-7-1905, Ruth Clare, born 2-7-1907, died 6-10-1986, James Horace (my dad) born 10-6-1909, died 8-25-1960, Charles Joseph (C.J.) born 8-7-1914, died 1-11-1978, and Horace Jr. (Nute) born 2-10-1916, died 11-10-2004.

DAD

*J*ames Horace McCaffrey came into this world October 8, 1909, (which happened to be on a Saturday) in Waco, Texas. He was the third child of Horace and Mary Lucinda Klepfer. He was killed in a head-on collision August 25, 1960, on the highway between Monahans and Pecos, Texas. He was fifty years, ten months, and seventeen days old. He is buried at Calvary Hill Cemetery in Dallas, Texas along with our mother Frances, and sisters Eileen and Mary Elise, and brothers Steve, Tommy and Don.

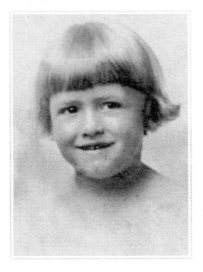

DAD – AGE 3

He spent some of his grade school years in Oak Cliff across the bridge from downtown Dallas. Once his brother, my Uncle Nute, came to visit us, and we drove over to the old neighborhood. Uncle Nute told us when they were young , dad took him to get a soda. There were some older boys present who were using foul language. My dad walked over and asked them to cool it because he had his little brother with him. Uncle Nute so appreciated this gesture. He told us our dad was a principled young boy who grew into a principled young man.

My grandfather, Pop and Mary Lucinda, moved his family up to the Milwaukee area. Dad went to Pio Nono High School in St. Francis, Wisconsin. He was the editor-in-chief of the semi-annual "The Pio Nonite" yearbook in 1927. I would like to add some articles my dad wrote in his yearbook:

SPIRIT OF COLUMBUS

Brave, courageous, bold to the point of recklessness, looking always to the future – that is the spirit of Columbus and the world he discovered.

Pioneers of civilization in the western world have always pictured Columbus as a long figure standing at the helm of his ship as he sailed from the staid conservation of the old world to seek laurels and engage in the daring conquest of the new.

This spirit of unflinching courage has lived on. Not because of itself, but for the qualities for which it stands. How could the memory of a man die who had the will to hold and carry out his opinions against the unbelief of the entire world? One who dared to attempt an enterprise which the greatest minds of the time had stamped as a fool-hearty exploit?

It is not only the accomplishment of courage and determination which is so remarkable, but the spirit behind it! The spirit that remains unshaken in the presence of the greatest trials.

By his undying belief in himself, by his unyielding spirit to compromise, and by his steadfast determination to continue in spite of all hardships, Columbus obtained his goal and discovered for man a new world.

Courage, steadfastness of character, faith and utter unselfishness are the dominant qualities of Columbus.

J.H.M. 28'

Here is another article written by our Dad:

FACULTY

Place trust in a boy and nine times out of ten, if he is a real American Boy, he will prove himself capable of the trust given to him.

The Faculty, to my mind, embraces the sentiments expressed in the above sentence. As a result, Pio Nono has a genuine spirit that is doing wonders in the scholastic and athletic field.

While trying to find some appropriate simile to illustrate the success of Pio Nono, as an institution, my mind is repeatedly brought back from its varied endeavors to life's greatest institution – the Home.

It has only recently come to me the full significance and magnitude of my father's love. It is he who shows me by example and gives me advice along those routes that lead to righteousness.

He is desirous that I embrace the virtues that make the perfect gentleman.

He listens to my tales of success and fortune and advises me what course to follow.

The value and love of that twinkle in his steady blue eyes, as I tell my part in some football game, has been interpreted by me as the outward expression of his faith in me. Now I realize the nature behind the stern, strict discipline, the sharp word and looks all given in the ecstasy of a father's love for his son.

Mothers are always present, their constant words of encouragement in success and failure ring in my ears and in times of defeat they resound as cheers to urge me to victory and the beautiful things in life; my powers of perception were rewarded somewhat earlier which resulted in the translation of my mother's looks and action.

Here I find it difficult to find a near suitable replication for the expression of sentiments.

Love is a Virtue – Mother is virtuous. She embodies all that is love.

The parents of Pio Nono, the faculty, embody to the fullest extent the qualities of both father and mother.

When one shows love, one is usually shown love in return. Where there is love – there is respect; where there is respect there is obedience; where there is obedience there is a union, and in union there is strength.

Pio Nono is strong because of this. How often have I noticed some homesick freshman be reconciled "to the world" by the endearing expressions of members of the faculty; and not infrequently I have seen one of the faculty speak to a boy as a father or mother would, urging him on to better and brighter things.

If all the faculties had this interest in their students many a boy would never leave school to battle his way in life, hampered by lack of proper preparation for life's struggles.

We, at Pio Nono are advancing incessantly towards a goal that will never be reached – for improvement provides for improvements.

J.H.M. 28'

Dad played left end on the Pio Nono football team. I would like to copy a description of this program from his yearbook:

FOOTBALL

Preparatory School Champions of Wisconsin – that exemplifies, in short, the goal attained and the record established by our wonder team of 27'. Our team reputed by pre-season dupe to be very formidable, justified, and even surpassed, if that were possible, all the flowery predictions made of it.

A glance over our record clearly shows the aggressiveness of this year's team. By decisively winning eight of our nine games and amassing a total of 214 points to our opponents 18, we have established an enviable record. A record surpassing any previous one made by Pio Nono elevens and one that may act as a target for future teams to shoot at.

A little thought given to the prestige and recognition obtained by some of our opponents serves only as an incentive to have greater respect for our own record. Among our opponents, four teams, Lincoln, West Allis, Marquette, and Campion, were of exceptionally high caliber. This foursome, although clearly outclassed against us, cut large swaths in high school competition, their record showing victories over some of the strongest teams in the state.

Our record can easily be explained by three things:

1st. The wonderful coaching and football knowledge obtained from our able coach, Erwin Wendt.

2nd. The absolute and whole-hearted harmony and support of the student body and the faculty.

3rd. The attitude of the team – the spirit of sacrifice or team spirit, so prevalent among the members of the squad was such, that no team, however great and well-organized it might be, could withstand or squelch it".

The following is the schedule and record made by our championship team of 27':

Sept 24	Pio Nono	13 Lincoln	0
Oct 1	Pio Nono	31 St John's	0
Oct 8	Pio Nono	19 West Allis	0
Oct 15	Pio Nono	6 St Catherine	12
Oct 22	Pio Nono	26 Oconomowoc	0
Nov 5	Pio Nono	39 Marquette	6
Nov 12	Pio Nono	27 St John's	0
Nov 19	Pio Nono	46 Racine	0
Nov 24	Pio Nono	7 Campion	0

The following is a description of Dad's performance on the football team:

JAMES MCCAFFREY

Mac proved an able running mate to Hayes, quick-thinking and a good pass receiver. Mac formerly lacked one thing, deadly tackling, to make him a star. He corrected that fault this year which made him master of his position and his graduation will leave a big hole to be filled.

I would also like to include the response of the coach about this team:

OUR COACHES CONCEPTION OF OUR TEAM

The Pio Nono football team of 1927 can be compared with an artist's portrayal of a work of art. His blending notes of music, or his harmony of color in a picture, represent the rhythm of action and the coordination of mind and body of our eleven man team.

Eleven men in a spirit of co-operative play, working according to the true code of sportsmanship, representing the traditional ideals of our school, naturally had to be successful.

But when we speak of success do we refer to a basis of wins and losses or do we turn to the moral benefits derived from a season of clean, wholesome competition? Each game we played added something new until the entire squad had learned the requirements of courage, co-operation, obedience, self sacrifice, and loyalty. They supplemented their learning with traits of character so that at all times they were cool under pressure, self confident in their undertakings, and whatever results they gained were realized by means of perseverance, patience and outstanding effort.

Summing up all these wonderful results gained during the season, we find the finished product, a gentleman. That was our success in 1927 because no matter where we played our players were always spoken of as gentlemen. Let's forget all the thrills that went with the game, let's forget all the wins we gained, but let's remember that Pio Nono's football team of 1927 was a group of gentlemen led by a gentleman leader, Captain Norbert Huennekens.

Personal Article by Coach Erwin E. Wendt

I want to mention the Doctor Salzmann Literary and Debating Society and our dad's role:

The Doctor Salzmann Literary and Debating Society may be compared to a plant, the seed of which was planted many years ago by Dr. Salzmann. Dad was the president of this group.

41

MOM AND DAD'S EARLY LIFE

*A*fter high school, dad went down to St. Mary's University in San Antonio. He played end on the football team. My mom, who was a student at Incarnate Word College, also in her first year, met dad at a get acquainted dance in the gym. She writes about this handsome young man from Milwaukee. She didn't forget him, and she found out weeks later he had not forgotten her either.

Several weeks went by. Mom and some of her girl friends drove over to St. Mary's and while there inquired about a certain Jim McCaffrey. Dad was out at the time. Then mom was called to the phone one day. It was dad! He asked her to a Friday night dance at St. Mary's. There was definitely something different about dad, so my mom wrote. He was quite serious about many things.

JIM AND FRANCES – 1929

So, their freshman year went by with football games, dances, a lot of studying, and a few dinners out when they had the money. At the end of the year, dad returned to Milwaukee and mom to Dallas.

Here is a letter dad wrote to our mom.

Dear Frances

What's the use? _____I can't express the sentiments and good wishes that I desire to, however, I will ask you to look through the noble things your Aunt Jeanette said about you, also Aunt Dot, and add what I think about you.

I was first attracted by your pep and open, carefree smile. _____ the attraction turned to interest in you after having a wonderful dance with you. It was not until we took that walk (you remember) that I came to realize how exceptional you were. The rest you know.

Frances, I have an ideal and you are the nearest to my ideal – this is saying more than you can imagine. It is saying all that I can say.

Red Head, I predict great happiness for you. I think I know somebody who will and can make you radiantly happy!

Truly,
Jim McCaffrey

Not a month went by, when mom received an invitation from dad to visit his family in Milwaukee. My grandmother and father agreed that mom could make the trip. She would travel with a girl friend, Helen Doran, to Chicago. Dad would meet her there and go on to Milwaukee with her. Dad's sister, Ruth, and his mother gave a nice

FRANCES MERON WILSON – 1928

43

luncheon in her honor. My mother had a great time and she said the McCaffrey family was so friendly and full of fun.

At the end of the summer, dad dropped by Dallas on his way back to St. Mary's to begin his sophomore year. Mom also was preparing to return to Incarnate Word to continue her study in music. She played the piano beautifully.

Dad told my mom that his father had forbidden him to return to school due to lack of finances. That did not deter him one bit, he was determined to make it. What did he do? Well, he rigged up a little tailor shop and had his business cards printed up. The students were only too happy to have someone press their clothes for less than the neighborhood cleaner charged.

Many times, my mom wrote, the Incarnate Word girls and their dates would go over to Breckinridge Park to enjoy a Sunday afternoon. It was under a certain big tree that dad proposed to her. We have been there many times on our visits to San Antonio. Dad would always tell the story like this, "A nut fell from the overhanging tree and hit me on the head, and when I came to I had asked Frances to marry me!"

Mom said her family became alarmed when she wrote home that she wanted to marry Jim McCaffrey. My grandmother's younger sister, Aunt Dorothy, was sent down from Dallas to break it up. It wasn't long however, until dad had actually sold Aunt Dot on the idea too.

One of the Incarnate Word Sisters called my dad to come over and discuss the situation. "What do you mean taking one of our girls?" "Please sister," dad said, "You are mistaken because one of your girls is going with me."

So, on Thanksgiving Day in 1929, mom and dad were joined in Holy Matrimony at Sacred Heart Cathedral in Dallas. Mom described it as a Solemn Nuptial Mass with Msgr. Diamond as celebrant, Msgr. Danglymeyer and Msgr. Nold as con-celebrants. Mary Beth Vogel and Uncle Monk O'Brien were the respective Bridesmaid and Best Man.

Grandmother O'Brien's house hosted the breakfast after

Mass. Aunts Dorothy and Jeanette prepared a lovely meal for everyone.

Off they went, to the Baker Hotel in Mineral Wells, for their honeymoon. My grandfather loaned them his Model T. Uncle Harry McCaffrey had paid the bill! What a nice surprise.

Soon, my dad decided to go on up to Milwaukee and find a job which he did. He then sent for our mother. Mom felt a little lonely with dad at work all day and off to classes some evenings. She had trouble cooking. She noticed that her mother-in-law cooked so well and so simply, so how come it was so difficult for her? Mom wrote that mainly she could never get everything cooked at the same time. If the meat was done, the potatoes weren't. She suspected that dad might have mentioned something to his mother because she soon asked them to move into a vacant room, paying room and board. Mom quietly blended on in to the kitchen helping to prepare the meals. She learned a lot.

The Milwaukee weather with snow piled high was a far cry from the South. My dad's two younger brothers, Uncles C.J and Nute, would take her out for walks in the snow.

Mom said she felt a little pang when she learned that she and dad would be moving to Louisville, Kentucky. Dad had some kind of office job there. It wasn't long until he called her one day to say how bored he was just sitting there, answering phones, picking up a pencil and filling an order. Finally, the manager gave him his first sales job in Evansville, Indiana.

She told us a few tales about life in Louisville. They had run up quite a dental bill, so as soon as dad received his check, they paid most of it off, leaving barely enough to live on. Dad walked the twelve blocks to and from work. On pay day, they splurged and shared a chicken dinner out at a nearby restaurant. Also, mom decided to do all the laundry. Having never starched before, she doused dad's entire shirt in the starch. He called from the office to say how embarrassing it was. Every time he moved, his shirt made crackling sounds to say nothing of how uncomfortable it was. Many times, later on, they laughed about this neophyte homemaker.

It was Christmas Eve in Louisville. Mom wrote that she and dad strolled through the streets hand in hand, enjoying the lights and store displays. She bought him a pair of house shoes and dad gave her a bottle of perfume. Somehow they just knew they both felt lonely being away from their families. Mom said she made up her mind that she would never feel that way again and by golly she didn't. Our mother possessed a determination unequaled to anyone I have ever known. That's the Irish spirit for you!

She relates that Christmas of 1930 was made special by a nice roast beef dinner, home -made cookies and candy.

You know that roast beef dinner she spoke of? Well, it became the traditional Sunday afternoon meal at the McCaffrey house and looks like it will remain so on thru the ages. It remains a favorite.

Mom was expecting her son, Jim, at this time. In fact, her doctor told her to take good care of herself, that she might not be able to carry a baby full term. He didn't know our mother, or any Irish woman for that matter. You see, you can never tell an Irish woman she can't do something! By golly, she will!

Before mom and dad left Louisville, my grandmother Wilson and great grandmother O'Brien paid them a visit. Grandmother O'Brien taught mom how to bake ham steak, potatoes, onions and carrots, all layered in a dish with milk added. I also make this dish from time to time. Mmm, think I'll make it this weekend.

THE START OF THE JIM MCCAFFREY FAMILY

It was early spring 1931 when mom and dad packed their belongings and headed for Evansville. Dad found a little apartment on the ground floor, and James Joseph McCaffrey was born on May 3, 1931. He was called Jimmy Joe. Mom said she was in the hospital for three weeks.

I would like to quote a beautiful sonnet her son Jim composed to our mother many years later:

A SONNET TO MY DEAREST LOVED
Of all the creatures that the world has seen,
One is, I think, the fairest of them all;
She reigns supreme, she rules in a great hall,
That hall, my heart, the castle of my queen.
Her treasury is from my person gleaned,
Though odd it is, its name is often called
By that dynamic word that has enthralled,
Deep love, sincere, abiding, and serene.
And with this greeting, may you be content
I pray, that some small love has been conferred
Upon so great a mother, and so blest;
For there is neither time nor an event
That offers greater chance for thanks to stir,
Than this, your day, when gratitude is stressed.

A Benedictine priest, Father James, assisted at St. Benedict's parish in Evansville. He became like one of the family. Mom said he and dad would have these long theological discussions. She would excuse herself and off to bed she went.

Soon, she could see the goodness in dad's heart as he reached out to help whomever. He began visiting the Orphanage. He came home one day and asked if they could adopt this darling little girl. Mom responded that while she would love to do this, they just might have more children of their own. Now, that was an under-statement! Seventeen kids later her family was complete!

Soon, my brother Patrick Quinlan McCaffrey (Patty Boy) was born August 5, 1932. Mom said he was a dark haired bundle of chubbiness. In fact, through the years, he always had that smile and chuckled a lot. If you mentioned Pat to our mother, she would just smile.

When Pat was two months old, a train ticket arrived in the mail for mom to visit the family in Dallas. She had been gone for three years.

FOUR GENERATIONS ! – 1932
GRANDMOTHER WILSON WITH JIM – MOM WITH PAT – GREAT
GRANDMOTHER JOHANNAH QUINLAN O'BRIEN

She so enjoyed the visit, showing off her two boys. She said Aunt Dot and Uncle Albert took her to a Texas--Oklahoma football game. It was time, however, to return home to Evansville and my mom said, "Tears rolled down my cheek as the train pulled out."

Times were not good and my dad got laid off from his job in Evansville. So his family packed up and returned to Milwaukee to look for work.

Dad's mother and father were so gracious and welcomed his family with open arms. His mom decided to fix a real Southern dish, some home-made chili. After several bites the whole bunch headed for the kitchen sink to get some water! Grandma Mary Lucinda began to laugh, and so did everyone else. She had put too much chili pepper into the chili. Mom wrote that it was from her that she got all this advice about cooking! If you make a fizzle of a dish, put a little nutmeg in it and call it a "cocktail." Her sense of humor was contagious. This showed up in my dad all the time.

Mom wrote that no work was found in Milwaukee, so they headed down South to Dallas. As they drove across the Texas border, dad got out and kissed the ground. After all, the depression was not so bad in Texas as in other places. In no time, dad was busy working again.

Mom appreciated the help she received from her mother in the case of her two boys. Dad, Jimmy Joe, and Paddy Boy had a little club in which no women were allowed (meaning my mom), and called it "The Three Wise Men." Mom said these were happy times. Aunt Dot and Uncle Albert took her and the children for rides. Jimmy Joe got his first haircut, and went from the whimsical blonde curls to the little man look.

Mary Elise was born January 18, 1934, and her older brothers were happy as could be. Mom wrote about her death, only eighteen months later, on June 28, 1935.

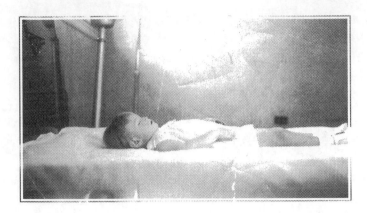

MARY ELISE MCCAFFREY – 18 MONTHS

According to her death certificate, the cause of death was Colitis. It was confirmed by our Uncle Dennis O'Brien, M.D. (I want to interject here that many years later I was out at Calvary Hill Cemetery looking for Mary Elise's grave and couldn't find it. I went into the office to discover that she was in a pauper's grave with no headstone. Oh no! We have to get her a headstone. So, with the help of my brothers and sisters she now has a lovely headstone with a little cherub angel asleep on the top edge. She is in Section E right next to the big Haggar monument.)

Mom said that the funds were low and she and dad still owed the hospital and the doctor for Mary Elise's care. Then, out of the blue, a letter came from dad's Company stating that he was to receive a retro-active raise to January...it was just enough to pay the bill. Mom wrote "how could we ever have doubted that Our Lord would take care of us?"

Dad was back as a salesman for Pittsburgh Plate Glass Company, and doing a good job according to mom. They were making friends and dad was becoming more active in his faith, becoming President of the Holy Name Society at Sacred Heart Cathedral.

Mom was expecting another baby in December. She prayed that God would send her another girl to take the place of Mary Elise, and so it happened that on December 5, 1935, my sister

50

JoAnne came into this world. Once again, mom said she and dad had little money, but lots of love.

I would like to share this funny story about my dad and JoAnne. This happened when she was a teenager. JoAnne was late getting dressed for a date. Her hair was still in curlers and she had a slip on. Dad decided to play a prank on her. He went out the back door and was going to ring the front door bell, pretending to be her date. Well, he stumped his toe on a rock, and was held up. Meanwhile, JoAnne's date arrived. She was told about dad's plan, so she threw open the door and said, "I know it's you daddy," but instead, it was her date! Dad came limping around the corner of the house about this time, and JoAnne was mortified!

Speaking of JoAnne, I'll just mention that when she was at Incarnate Word College, she belonged to a Confraternity of Christian Doctrine. She was to represent her college at the national convention in Buffalo, New York. It just so happened that dad was to speak at this same convention. JoAnne told us that she would never forget how her dad stood at that podium, so dignified yet humble. He captured the attention of all by the interesting material, as well as his informal delivery interspersed with humor.

Dad loved the company of the priests. Aunt Dot and Uncle Albert had Saturday dinners out at their house for the priests and their friends. My grandmother baby sat the children. Mom also enjoyed her nights out.

Moving along now with this family, John Charles (Skippy) was born, according to mom, one bright July 9, 1937, in the morning. My dad's parents came for a visit to help out. My brother, Pat, told me that Skip got the name because he would sort of skip along everywhere.

Next in line was yours truly, Ursula Kathleen, born October 20, 1938. Mom said I was a blue eyed, chubby girl, who was content and easy to care for. As it turned out, I look more like my mom than the rest of my sisters. I watched her a lot and took on some of her characteristics, like her love of writing, her energy, and music. She played music and I was always singing music. I was dressed in blue in honor of the Blessed Mother. My little brothers and sisters called me slasla because it was too hard to pronounce Ursula. (I'll write more about me later on.)

Here is a poem mother wrote about our father:

OUR JIM

Have you ever known a man whose fate
It was to march fast step through life
Amid the clarion of never ending strife?
His wife and children recalling
"He was mainly good," they'd say,
"And couldn't help but be a certain way."
When others slowed or took their ease
And lingered enjoyingly,
He would press enduringly;
Ever on. Jim strode and fought
Looking for what he thought was right,
Loving, living, as best he might.

Angela Marie was to follow me, taking her place on March 3, 1940, as mom wrote, another pretty little girl, another student for Ursuline Academy. Angela and I were taken to the Ursuline Convent where special prayers were said on our behalf. You see, Saints Angela and Ursula founded the Ursuline Sisters.

Meanwhile, dad was busier than ever. I remember several years later that the Bishop of Dallas would periodically call my dad for some assignment. Dad would pick up a man from the mental hospital, bring him to our house for a night or two, while he arranged a job for him. Then he received calls from other Bishops and was sent out on assignments to bring people back to their Faith or for others reasons.

Here is an article from the newspaper regarding the Serra Club:

HISTORY OF STRONG GROWTH MARKS SERRA CLUB OF

DALLAS

By Daniel Kennelly

DALLAS. Half a century has passed since the Serra Club of Dallas first began its mission of fostering priestly and religious vocations, and since then both Dallas and the club have witnessed dramatic growth and change.

In 1948, the year of the club's official charter, less than 10% of Dallas' approximately 350,000 citizens were Catholic, but today the Dallas Diocese is over half a million Catholics strong.

The Serra Club of Dallas, the first of its kind in the area, has had a history of strong growth as well.

From that single chapter came the eight metroplex chapters and more than 400 Serrans that continue their mission of promoting vocations today.

What started in Seattle in 1934 as a group of Catholic men who gathered to discuss Christian values later became Serra International, a worldwide laymen's movement for the promotion of priestly and religious vocations. Dallas' Serra club had its origins in this international organization.

In 1946, recalled Jerome J. Crane, a charter member, he was planning the monthly speaker for the fourth-degree Knights of Columbus luncheon when he got a call from James McCaffrey, the secretary-treasurer of the National Council of Catholic Men. Mr. McCaffrey asked Mr. Crane if he had confirmed a speaker for the next month.

Mr. Crane said he had not set the program yet, and Mr. McCaffrey told him "cancel it and don't plan on any more fourth-degree luncheons. Bishop Lynch has other plans, and we'll tell you more about it later."

A month later, Mr. Crane was called to a meeting with Dallas Bishop Joseph Patrick Lynch and five other prominent Dallas Catholics. They discussed forming a local chapter of Serra International, a growing service organization.

EILEEN FRANCES MCCAFFREY

Moving on now – Dad bought his first home on 4427 Bowser Avenue. We moved into this house May 31, 1941. My sister, Eileen Frances (Leenie) was born June 1, 1941. Later on Eileen was one of the children who accompanied dad to Heaven. I remember her as being so sweet and thoughtful. She loved the Nancy Drew books.

If one of us older kids was away at camp, or school, on our birthday, dad always called us long distance, and all the little ones lined up to wish us well. Each child had something to share, that is, everyone but Eileen. She no sooner said "hello" and then would break into tears. She sure had a sensitive heart.

We were now in Holy Trinity Parish. Dad organized the first Holy Name Society and became its president. He joined the Knights of Columbus and soon became the secretary, then treasurer, of the National Council of Catholic Men. Seems to me his heart was plum full of the love for God and his fellow man.

His love for his family was also very great. He always returned home from his business trips early, and we were always surprised. He gathered us around him to share stories about his journeys. I remember dropping him off at the Dallas Train Terminal. Occasionally, when picking him up, I would walk on in to the track and wait for his train to arrive. What excitement to see the big engine pull up.

Later on, he would leave on Wednesday of Holy Week and head for the Trappist Monastery in Conyers, Georgia with Abbot Augustine, for his yearly retreat. His return was an added joy in the celebration of the risen Lord on Easter Sunday. Yes, we were happy that Jesus finally completed His mission on this earth rising up to join His Father and we could rejoice that our dad was refreshed in body, mind and soul. I could see the light in his eyes.

My brother, Michael Vincent, was next on the family agenda, born November 18, 1942. He has big brown eyes. He went missing one day and was found sleeping under his bed. I was four at the time. The Sister Provential of the Daughters of Charity was visiting our grade school, from Paris, France. Michael was chosen to present flowers to her all dressed up in cowboy attire.

My mom wrote that it was at this time that dad went with Southwestern Life Insurance Company. Herschel Ingram encouraged him. What a blessing. Seems to me the more kids we had the more insurance dad sold!

I have to tell this story about dad. One day he was at work and was in Mr. Costello's office. It just so happened he had one black sock and one brown sock on. Mr. Costello said, "Come on Jim, we've got some shopping to do, you have to dress well in this insurance business." So, he bought my dad some new duds.

On one occasion dad had a client come by interested in buying insurance. Dad was so honest that he recommended the client see another company because that type insurance would better suit his needs. So the client was referred to a representative from that other company. You know that old saying "What goes around comes around?" The other insurance agent was so impressed that he in turn referred 10-15 people back to dad for their policies.

I have a vague memory of the time when Lyndon Johnson was the Majority Leader in the Senate. He assisted our dad in the clearance of the "Annuity Program". Dad's first big client was the Daughters of Charity hospital system.

Around the time Jesuit High School opened. Father James Buckley S.J. became a friend to our family. Mom said he was the first Jesuit she had ever met and he really impressed her.

Donald Anthony (Don Juan) joined the family on June 30, 1945. He was named after Father Donald Hartnett, and Father Anthony Daly. Mom said that Father Daly called one day asking to speak to Tony. Mom responded that there wasn't anyone here by that name. "Well, there better be," he said, "because Jim told me he named one of his kids after me."

I will mention that years later, February 15, 1989, our brother Don passed away as a result of diabetic ketoacidosis. He was interred at Calvary Cemetery alongside several of his brothers and his sister.

MOM AND DON

Here is a letter written to me from one of Don's friends dated March 3, 1989:

Dear Mrs. Heuiser,

Don McCaffrey and I met 5 or 6 years ago on a Dallas public tennis court. I was looking for a game of tennis and he offered to take me on. I think he won that first match.

We were good friends ever since. He would call to play tennis and once we were on the court, it was all business. For a while it bothered me, his earnest focus to beat me. But after a while, I realized that was just his way, certainly not a personal attack. He always expected me to play my very best, otherwise he'd let me know, in no uncertain terms. Ultimately, we had a lot of fun trying to get the best from each of us.

When congress legislated his occupation, a Polygraph Examiner, practically out of existence, it was a big blow. He was like a fish out of water. I thought he was enjoying his part time work like teaching drivers training and teaching tennis.

I lost regular contact with Don around the middle of November. I deeply regret not being able to push aside my personal life for an occasional phone call or visit.

I cherished Don's friendship and I will miss him greatly.

Sincerely,
David Boyd

Another letter written to our mother dated April 21, 1989:

Dear Mrs. McCaffrey,

Please accept my condolences about the untimely death of your fine son Don.

We first met as classmates at Jesuit during 1960-1963 where Don well earned the "wittiest" award. I didn't see too much of him during his time at Texas A&M, but we had periodic contact thereafter through other classmates. You may remember a couple of times when I came to your home on Gooding Dr to watch football games with Don.

Don and I were together a lot in 1982-1983 working on our high school 20 year reunion. He was the Master of Ceremonies and provided us with many hours of laughter and fun memories.

I will miss his political analyses, his jokes and laughter, lunches at the Egyptian Lounge, discourses about polygraph and tennis tips. My life has been enriched by knowing Don and I will pray for the happy repose of his soul.

Sincerely,
Chris Bird

A postcard to our mother from Rome Dated March 29, 1989:

Dear Mrs. Mccaffrey,

Just got a note from Pat Koch about Donny. Will remember him in my Mass. Strong backs tote the cross right down to the wire, not far behind Jesus Himself. Far from fatalistic, Faith is what gives the Cross it's meaning – and its beauty, too, when suffered with love. But you know all that better than I do.

Lordy, what a long time it's been since the early fifties back on Oak Lawn ! I've been thru Dallas since several times, but only for overnight visits. Meanwhile, my love to all the kids, grandkids, great-grandkids and anyone else whose memory can reach back 35 years.

Your faith has been one of my retreat stories down thru the years, and there are people all over the world who thank God for you and it.

Much Love in the Lord,
Jack Vessels, SJ

Robert Stephen (Stevie) came to us on August 18, 1946. He was Mom and Dad's 10th living child. (Mary Elise and Charles Joseph were previously deceased.) The movie and book "Cheaper by The Dozen" with Clifton Webb came out about this time. Father Patrick Peyton of the Family Rosary Hour came by to join us in our family Rosary. He gave each one of us an Irish horn Rosary. Steve also accompanied dad to Heaven later on.

Margaret Ann graced us with her birth June 15, 1948. I so

enjoyed helping my mom care for her and all the other little ones. How fun to share the holidays, birthdays and just day by day activities.

Mom told us about a surprise baby shower for her next baby. Aunt Dot and Aunt Ella arranged it all. It was held at Marie Saunders house and everybody she knew came. So, Christine Marie (Christabel) arrived December 27, 1949, in grand style and took her place in the family. Her birth brought extra Christmas joy into the whole family. She was so sweet and loving as she grew.

The following November 30, 1950, my mom had a term still-born baby girl named Dorothy Genevieve. I was in the sixth grade. My dad told me about this several days before she went to the hospital, so I could be of extra help to her. I watched her carefully and never detected the true sorrow she was feeling. I prayed to the Blessed Mother for her as the Blessed Mother knew all about carrying sorrow in her heart. I stayed home from school the day mom went to the hospital. I was to look after my brothers and sisters. That night, supper was prepared and all were seated at the twelve foot long table. Aunt Dorothy and Mary Beth dropped by to see how things were getting on. Well, everything was fine.

This reminds me that once when I was in the eighth grade, mom joined dad on a business trip, the first time ever. We were all so excited. Dad left some money with me for groceries. It was no problem to plan the meals. I just continued my mom's usual dishes. When they returned home I had $5.00 left over, so I placed the $5 bill on a platter, and asked mom and dad to have a seat in the living room. We had a presentation to make. So, we presented dad with the left over money. They gave us all big hugs.

Thomas Christopher (Tom Tom) arrived on March 2, 1952. (He, along with Eileen, and Steve and dad were killed on August 25, 1960, in a head on collision in West Texas.) Tommy was eight at the time of his death. When he was a bit younger, I was told he was forever making long distance phone calls to his older brothers and sisters. Of course, this wasn't noticed until the phone bill arrived. Tommy had those little freckles across his nose and dad called them "angel kisses." He had a cowlick on top of his head that always managed to stick straight up. Mom told us that Tommy had dearly loved his father. How special that he accompanied his dad to Heaven.

A classmate of Tom, Joyce Meyer at the time, was his partner for First Holy communion procession. Sister Henry kept trying to smooth down his cowlick. He fidgeted a lot and couldn't keep his hands folded right. She mentioned those freckles across his nose.

January 14, 1954, Philip (Philly) Dennis came to join our family. He was the 14th living child of my mom and dad. Three children were deceased.

Philip was named after dad's college buddy, Dr. Philip Rodriquez, and Uncle Dennis O'Brien. Of course, we all were named after a patron saint too.

I remember well the day of Philip's Baptism. Bishop Gorman performed the ceremony. Dad invited the Bishop to our house for a reception afterwards. It was time for the little ones to go to bed so Bishop Gorman came back to their beds, knelt down and said night prayers with each one. We were so honored to have the Bishop visit us.

MCCAFFREY FAMILY – 1954 (JIM AND PAT ABSENT)

25ᵀᴴ WEDDING ANNIVERSARY

JIM AND FRANCES MCCAFFREY 25TH WEDDING
ANNIVERSARY WITH BISHOP GORMAN

*D*ad made plans to celebrate the 25th anniversary of his marriage to our mother. Thanksgiving Day, 1954, the celebration took place at Holy Trinity Church. Mom wore her lovely black dress, and added a pink scarf around the neck, and a pink hat to match. She also wore her gloves. Angela and Eileen went with Mom to the dressmaker across the street to have that pink scarf added.

Several hundred invitations went out to friends, relatives, Bishops, priests and sisters. Bishop Gorman presided with Father Carl Vogel, our cousin, as celebrant. Father Buehler S.M. gave the sermon. Mom said his sermon was so inspirational it made her cry. She said it was as if she was listening to someone else's life. A lovely breakfast followed at the Melrose Hotel for many of the out of town guests and the Bishop. I so enjoyed the camaraderie of all those friends of the family.

An open house was planned for 4:00 p.m. Our house was filled with flowers, gifts, and many telegrams. My brother Pat was in the Marine Corp and was in Korea. He sent mom and dad a beautiful set of china, which arrived intact.

Here is a letter written by Fr Ralph Dyer, S.M. on November 28, 1954:

Dear Jim and Frances,

This is to let you know that Brother John and I arrived safely home after a most enjoyable Thanksgiving Day with you in Dallas. There are many memories of that day with you in Dallas. There are many memories of that day that I'll treasure for a long time--- the glorious Mass, the sermon, the clergy and religious assembled, your children. I've never seen a more polite boy than Michael, and Christine and Margaret Ann are God's prettiest creatures. In short, I don't know when I've had a better time. Thank you so much for letting me be with you that day.

I should like to write Pat in Korea and detail some of the day's happenings. I was certainly happy to hear what he had done for you. Good boy.

My Mass at Jesuit was for both of you-----and I'm going to offer another in January for you. It's all I can do to show you how much I enjoyed the trip.

Pray for my retreat in Brownsville next week. I'm sure it will succeed if only one of your children would keep it prayerfully in mind.

Father Ralph, S.M.

DAD'S LAST YEARS

I would like to continue this story about my Dad until the time he was called home.

Dad went to San Antonio to celebrate JoAnne's graduation from Incarnate Word College, May 1958. It was there he collapsed in the lobby of Santa Rosa Hospital from a really bad heart attack. Joanne was on staff at Santa Rosa completing her internship for medical technology. She was able to visit him every day. His stay lasted 30 days. Upon his recovery, he stopped smoking, revised his diet, and started exercising. Mom told me he was like the pied piper, walking around the neighborhood with all of his kids in tow.

Now, three months later, in August of 1958, he came to see me. I was a novice in the Society of Catholic Medical Missionaries. (I'll write more about this part of my life later in another story.) Anyway, when I walked into the parlor, I noticed that dad's face looked a little swollen, especially around the eyes. Oh, I thought, I can tell he has been sick, and my stomach sank a little. Outwardly I welcomed him with a big smile and a hug. We had a great visit. He shared so many stories about my brothers and sisters. Mom was doing well too. A couple of times he reached into his pocket for a little pill holder, which contained his tiny nitro pills. He popped one into his mouth and didn't comment to me anything about what he was feeling. I knew he was having some chest pain, and I raised him silently to the Lord.

He always shared some spiritual teaching with me. This time he asked me if I had been assigned to kitchen duty yet. "No, not yet", I said. Well, he said, "when you go among the pots and pans, think of Jesus like the Little Flower Therese, and offer up the little actions of the day." "Ok dad", I said. The time did come and as I stepped into the kitchen, by golly, I remembered dad's message to me. Thank you Holy Spirit for that gift.

Dad always referred to Our Lord as "The Boss". So, just as he was leaving, he asked me to go into the chapel and ask the "Boss" for a favor. "You bet dad", I said. He said, "Will you ask the Boss if he could please give me two more years? I need to prepare your mother." He mentioned several other matters that needed attention. So, as dad left I felt like always the pang in my heart. I'll interject here, the pain I felt was like the one when I left home. The pain I felt when, later on, I left for Africa and then again when I had to leave my dear friends in Africa. It really does hurt. Always, whenever I would feel this pain, I would offer it up to Jesus. Mom and dad always told us to "offer our little sacrifices to Jesus." It never lasted very long as I was always getting on with the next present moment.

I went right to the chapel, knelt down, and said, "Boss, my daddy needs a favor from you. If it be your holy will, will you give him two more years? Thank you in advance." The tears were pouring down my cheeks. So, I offered the tears to Jesus. He wants us to offer our whole life to Him, the rainy days as well as the sunshine days, whatever the present moment dictates.

I found these few words about God and His plan: "But God has a plan. Instead of corruption, there is going to be honesty. Instead of indulgence, there is going to be sanctity. Instead of war, there is going to be peace. And all of this is going to happen because God is great and God has a plan. We are all part of that plan and, by golly, Isaiah says we had better get in step with the Boss." This so reminds me of my father. Mom and dad both spoke to us periodically about God's Providence. "His Providence rises before the dawn."

(Sure enough, two years later on August 25, 1960, dad left this world for the Heavenly Kingdom. How merciful of the Lord to bring some of his children along with him.)

In 1958, dad won the Grand Challenge Award from Southwestern Life Insurance Company. This was the highest honor conferred on a salesman. Mom wrote about this. Mr. Woods, the President, introduced dad to the convention with many words of praise for his work. Mom thought, "Could this be my husband they were all looking at?"

I would like to copy an article written in the Southwestern Insurance Company News Report:

MCCAFFREY, FULLER EARN COMPANY'S TOP AWARDS

"In the stately atmosphere of the International Room of New Orleans' Roosevelt Hotel, Southwestern Life's 1959 Agency Convention reached a splendorous climax when President James Ralph Wood presented SWL's top awards to the Company's most outstanding agents of 1958 and 1959.

More than 450 agents, wives, and special guests attended the festive awards banquet, concluding event of the two-day SWL Convention June 18th and 19th.

SWL's top honors for 1959 were earned by James H. McCaffrey and Richard G Fuller, both of Dallas, Ned B. Henry of Fort Worth, and Robert H Hartley of Tulsa.

JIM MCCAFFREY

To Jim McCaffrey went the Company's 1959 Grand Challenge Award for leading the entire SWL agency force in volume of paid-for business during 1958. He also was the winner of two other top honors – The Presidency of the Southwestern Life Club and the award for the Largest Amount of Premium Credit. In addition, Jim was among the 30 winners of Company Quality Awards of 1959.

As SWL's 1959 grand champion, Jim McCaffrey accomplished what many would believe to be the near impossible; he came off a hospital bed to set a blazing production pace that carried him to his top awards. In May of last year, he was stricken with a heart attack from which he later recovered to lead SWL field force in production for three consecutive months – September,

65

October and November. His great individual performance in 1958 during which he produced $ 3,066.019 of Club paid-for business was one that marked him as a true champion.

Jim has specialized to a considerable extent in pension trust cases but has not neglected the ordinary field. His paid production last year included $825.983 of business on individual lives.

Following 13 years of sales experience with the Pittsburgh Plate Glass Co. in Dallas, Jim joined Southwestern Life in November 1943. A life member of both TLRT and MDRT, he has qualified eleven years for the MDRT (Million Dollar Round Table) membership, including 1959. He is a member of the Company's Million Club and Top Club.

Mom said as she sat with dad at the awards banquet, she could only gaze in loving wonderment at this man, her husband. He was Jim, the missionary, as he reached out to souls in need. He was Jim, her loving husband, Jim, the father, Jim, the friend, Jim, the businessman, and Jim, the layman with a deep love of God first and foremost. What do you say of a man who had such convictions about his faith, and lived up to them, but that he was, as my mom called him "one of God's noble men?"

I am now ready to tell the story of my dad's last days on this earth. It was August, 1960. Dad had some business in West Texas, and decided to take a few children with him, Eileen, Margaret Ann, Stevie, Tommy and Philip. Mom told us how they called each night and were having such a good time.

August 25, 1960, at 2:30 p.m. dad was driving the Volkswagen and cruising along a deserted West Texas highway (Hwy 80) between Monahans and Pecos. A 53' Oldsmobile was coming in the opposite direction with three passengers in it. The car had a blow-out and it veered over head long into dad's car. The State Highway Patrol officers reported this accident to be one of the worst in the Pecos area. Dad, Tommy, and Stevie died right way. Eileen lived several hours. Margaret Ann and Philip survived the crash.

Then followed the unfortunate duty of someone to tell my

mom about the accident. She wrote about this later. There was a knock on the door and in walked Bishop Dangylmeyer. The Bishop mentioned an accident but mom said she knew dad was a good driver, she didn't think it was serious. Then she recognized Mr. Davenport and Mr. Swift from Southwestern Life. She knew it was serious after all. After some time, she now understood what my dad meant when he would explain this or that about the finances, his business etc. Yes, he had been preparing her.

My mom said God in His goodness sustained her through the long ordeal of suffering. She said it seemed so natural that dad should have the company of his own beloved children to go along with him.

I was a professed Sister by this time, in Philadelphia, preparing to start Nurses Training. Nine o'clock, on the night of August 25th, I was still in the chapel when I was informed of the bad news.

So, I packed my bag and took the next flight to Dallas, arriving in the early morning hours. I stayed quietly beside my mother, day after day. I wasn't there for the viewing of the bodies at the funeral home. I was told that there were two separate prayer services to handle the crowds.

After the funeral and burial, mom and I were flown to Pecos, Texas, where Margaret Ann and Philip were hospitalized. Mother hired a night nurse to care for them from 7p to 7a. She and I were there during the day. Philip was six and Margaret Ann was twelve. I remember buying several finger puppets at the dime store. I spent hours under Philip's big crib bed, talking and playing with those puppets. I had different voices for each one. All he saw were these little characters.

It was soon time for me to return to Philadelphia, to begin Nurses Training. When I left my mother, I felt that pain of loss once again.

I want now to include the various newspaper articles and letters of condolences pertaining to my dad and brothers and sister.

Letter from Mr. John P. Costello dated August 26, 1960:
Mr. F. Gordon O'Neill
2122 Kidwell Street
Dallas, Texas

Dear Gordon,

It was only after my telephone conversation with you that I began to realize that I had agreed to a responsibility that I am not qualified to discharge. I now realize that it would be an impossible task for me to put my thoughts and feelings toward Jim McCaffrey on paper.

It would probably be unnecessary for me to say, particularly to our mutual friends, that in my humble opinion he was one of the finest fathers, husbands and business associates that I have ever known in all my life, and I would be the first to admit that I have been very fortunate in having had the privilege of knowing and associating with some mighty fine men. I would be less than truthful if I did not readily admit, like hundreds of other men and women in all walks of life, that he had a profound influence for good on my own life.

Jim was certainly one of the most unusual people that I have ever known. His life in some ways made one doubt psychological principles that have more or less been accepted as fact, certainly in some degree, for instance, the instinct for self-preservation, the instinct to acquire and the fear of the unknown – the man just did not have them.

The acquisition of worldly goods, for instance, was never one of his objectives, and I believe he had as little fear of death as anyone I have ever met outside the religious life. Actually, I have never encountered such a simple, deep-seated faith in God as Jim possessed. Nothing could ever shake his firm conviction that the "Boss", as he often referred to Our Lord, understood all his problems better than he and even if he had not been informed of the solution, there was never any doubt in his mind that the "Boss" had the solution and at the proper time he would understand it.

He never allowed the distractions and complexities of his life as a business man, and he was a good business man as well as a good provider for his family, to switch the spotlight of his mind from his simple morning offering, which to my knowledge he never failed to make. Jim would arise in the morning with one aim and objective for the day and that was that he wanted to do everything that he should do according to the "Boss'" plan and will and not be influenced by his own desires or worldly pleasures. I imagine he closed each day with a self analysis and check-up to see if he had to the best of his ability carried out the "Boss'" wishes.

Of course, as everyone knows, he probably spent (and I will change the word spent to invested) more time and energy to helping others than he did to the solution of his own problems, but it seemed that his faith was always well-founded and some way or another everything would work out just like he thought it would.

I can remember back 17 years ago when he was leaving his salaried job where he certainly had a degree of security, to go into the life insurance business – a business he knew very little about – but even then he had very definite ideas of what life should mean to all of us and what we were put here for. Even though it was hard in the early days when he was getting started in a new business, he never let discouragement or disappointments shake his faith. He had not been in the business long until naturally he found out it was a very competitive business and he learned he was going to seek business that some of his good friends were also seeking and that there would be deals that would come up where he would learn of bitter controversy among some of his good friends over business that each friend was sincere in their feeling that they were justly entitled to the business. And, here, Jim might be credited with bringing a new thought to many of us who had been in the business a long time, because the only controversy you could get him in was to get him to agree that he was justly entitled to the business or at least to participate in it with you, and you would really find out that what he wanted was to withdraw completely and give it to the other fellow no matter who was involved.

The good things that I could truthfully and sincerely say about Jim McCaffrey would fill a book if I had time to recall and look back

over the past 17 years that I have known him. So, my closing obser-
vation would be that he was one guy who never forgot the "Boss"
and nothing will ever convince me that the "Boss" will ever forget
him.

Gordon, you can use any part of this that will serve your pur-
pose, and edit it as you wish. In the interest of time, it had to be
roughly typed.

With kindest personal regards, I am

Sincerely yours,

John P.Costello, C.L.U.

The Dallas Chapter, National Conference of Christians and Jews wrote the following to honor our dad:

In Appreciation of the Life Service of
JAMES H. MCCAFFREY
Dynamic Personality, Devoted Husband and Father,
Dedicated Churchman, Servant of His
Fellow Man

WHEREAS, Almighty God in His infinite wisdom has seen fit to call James H. McCaffrey to His heavenly reward at the earthly age of 50, creating a void in the ranks of men of good will in Dallas, in Texas and in the nation : and

WHEREAS, James H. McCaffrey loved and served his fellow man without regard or restriction as to religious distinction, nationality, background, race or creed, but as a brother, and by his actions set an example for his fellows : and

WHEREAS, James H. McCaffrey gave unreservedly of his time and talents to many worthwhile civic and welfare causes, contributing wise counsel, mature judgment and distinguished leadership to a wide range of organizations : and

WHEREAS, the educational program for good will and civic cooperation of the National Conference of Christians and Jews had the dedicated interest, unflagging support, and dynamic leadership of James H. McCaffrey, first through service as a member of the Southwestern Division Staff, then for many years as advisor to the Southwestern Division Director on matters of Catholic cooperation with the approval of the Bishop of the Diocese of Dallas-Fort Worth and the Archbishop of the Archdiocese of San Antonio, then for many years as a member of the Board of the Dallas Chapter of the Conference :

Therefore, we, the members of the Board of the Dallas Chapter, National Conference of Christians and Jews, assembled in meeting in Dallas on September 8, 1960, do hereby unanimously adopt this resolution of gratitude for the rich life, of unselfish service of James H. McCaffrey to his fellow man, express our deep sense of loss in his passing at the height of his career, and extend to his widow and family our assurance that his memory will live in our hearts; and instruct the Co-Chairman of the Dallas Chapter, National Conference of Christians and Jews, to sign this statement in our behalf and deliver a copy of it to the family of James H. McCaffrey, to the press, and to the National Office of the National Conference of Christians and Jews as our joint expression.

Thomas C. Unis   Louis Tobian   Angus G. Wynne, Jr.
Co-Chairman   Co-Chairman   Co-Chairman

September 8, 1960
Dallas, Texas

I recently found more statements from some of our friends submitted after dad's death. I will now add them:

STATEMENT OF ARTHUR C. HUGHES:
Jim McCaffrey had strong faith. He trusted in the Lord, and performed great personal charities for people, the record of which must remain confidential. They are written only in the Book of Life.

He used to come to my house for breakfast every week or so. We would talk over what he felt he had to do. He was with me one morning a week or so before he was killed.

He liked to be with people he loved, most of all with his wonderful children, all of whom he taught to pray in the recital at home of the family rosary.

Long before Pope Pius XI used the phrase "Catholic Action," Jim fulfilled the old term "Lay Apostle." He had a great zeal, and a deep reverence for the priesthood and the religious life of Brothers and Sisters.

What he did cannot all be told, but this much should be written in the record. He and John Malone persuaded Bishop Lynch to let them start the Serra Club of Dallas. Jim also was a pioneer in the start and development of the Confraternity of Christian Doctrine.

And Jim did "seek first the Kingdom of God," not only for his family, but for great numbers of others. He was active in many organizations and other efforts to spread and intensify the Kingdom of God in the hearts of others. To list all of these, even if I knew all of them, would take much more space than can be provided. As an example, however, I can say that he worked long and diligently to begin and foster the lay apostolate in our diocese through the Council of Catholic Men. In fact, on one occasion, I accompanied him on a trip to Washington D.C., and a meeting of the National Conference of Catholic Men there in order that we might come back to our diocese and try to put into practice at least some of the things we learned for the good of souls.

In all of Jim's endeavors, his humility and respectful obedience was notable. He always realized that the lay apostolate had to be subservient to the Ordinary (Bishop) and pastors of the diocese and therefore placed himself in their command when the cause of souls was concerned.

In short, Jim McCaffrey lived his life to carry out the command of Our Lord to "preach the gospel to every creature" by word, by work and by example.

STATEMENT OF BISHOP THOMAS K. GORMAN:

May I express my appreciation for what my friend, Jim McCaffrey, did for God and souls. His was an individual type of lay apostolate.

He sacrificed much in time away from his business and from

his intensely loved family to go after sheep that were lost all over the United States.

Under my predecessor, Bishop Lynch, he pioneered works of Catholic Action from which we have profited spiritually and socially.

The only way I can thank him is to keep remembering him, his deceased children and his bereaved wife and children in my Masses. This I shall do.

STATEMENT OF ST PAUL'S HOSPITAL:

Catholic Hospital sisters in many parts of the nation have lost a true friend and champion with the death of Jim McCaffrey.

Not only had he pioneered in the development of pension and insurance plans for many Catholic Hospitals, but three of his children have chosen the Catholic hospital apostolate for their work.

Mr. McCaffrey's interest in these institutions extended far beyond purely business relationships. Indeed, he was a sincere friend and trusted advisor whose counsel will be sorely missed by many hospital sisters.

Sister Mary Helen Neuhoff
Administrator, St Paul Hospital

STATEMENT OF MRS. ALBERT A. FABER:

People who knew Jim McCaffrey casually, spoke of him as a most likable person, friendly, fun loving, good natured and a hard worker for the betterment of civil and religious affairs. When there was a job to be done, the various organizations never failed to call upon him for help, both physically and financially and never was he known to turn them down.

But few people knew the real Jim McCaffrey as I did. He was too modest to let people know the real Jim. Being an aunt of his wife, I was very closely associated with the McCaffrey family and if Jim had a hobby, I would say it was doing good for the people who really needed help – the people whose troubles were such that organizations could not help. There was no distance too far nor hour too late for Jim to go to anyone in trouble. Most of his really good deeds were of such a personal nature that only his wife and perhaps a very few close friends knew of them. He had a deep pity for anyone in trouble.

Jim was most charitable, not only in a financial way but in the true meaning of the word charity as taught by our religion, namely being charitable to his fellow man by counseling, not condemning, him for his wrong doing. His help was not confined to people in Dallas, nor people of his own faith, but to people of all faiths and in all cities. I have known him to fly, at his own expense, many, many times to California, Florida, New York and many other States to help someone in need, sometimes people he didn't know, but who were relatives or close friends of friends of his. These cases were to help someone who was either trodding or on the verge of straying the straight and narrow.

The following is a Memoriam from the Chairman of the Million Dollar Roundtable:

IN MEMORIAM
WITH A DEEP SENSE OF LOSS, WE HONOR AND PAY
TRIBUTE TO THE MEMORY OF OUR BELOVED MEMBER
JAMES H. MCCAFFREY
HIS FINE CHARACTER, TRUE WORTH AND HIGH INTEGRITY
WON FOR HIM THE RESPECT AND AFFECTION OF THE
COMMUNITY IN WHICH HE LIVED. HIS FELLOW MEMBERS OF
THE MILLION DOLLAR ROUND TABLE OF THE NATIONAL
ASSOCIATION OF LIFE UNDERWRITERS, AND ALL WHO
KNEW HIM, GREATLY MOURN HIM.
THEREFORE: BE IT RESOLVED, THAT THIS MEMORIAL BE
ADOPTED AS A TOKEN OF SORROW WHICH THE MILLION
DOLLAR ROUND TABLE HAS SUSTAINED IN HIS PASSING,
AND THAT THIS MEMORIAL BE SPREAD UPON THE RECORDS
OF THE MILLION DOLLAR ROUND TABLE AND A COPY
THEREOF BE PRESENTED TO HIS FAMILY AS AN
EXPRESSION
OF HEARTFELT SYMPATHY.

I would like to share a testimony given by our sister, Eileen Frances McCaffrey, who accompanied our dad to Heaven. The following words were written by Eileen in the September, 1959 issue of TheLogos, the Incarnate Word College News:

"Spiritually I am here to strengthen my relationship with God. Secondly, by the intellectual curriculum established for me, I shall grow in wisdom and grace, and thus learn, know and understand what is being taught. This is very important for the happiness of a person. To use the intellectual faculties God has given one, is the most effective way of thanking Him."

The article goes on to say that these words of Eileen typify her wonderful view of life. She has left behind a memory that makes each of her friends and acquaintances feel fortunate to have known her. Before making her final act of consecration as a Sodalist, Eileen discussed with her Sodality counselor a point from a lecture given by the director of the Sodality, Rev. Thomas French. The lecture made such an impression on her that she remarked to her counselor, "I must always try to become better so that anyone with whom I come in contact will love Jesus and Mary more."

Sodalists remember her ready willingness to help and her faithfulness in doing well anything she set her mind to. She always saw to it that the rosary was recited each night in Dubois Hall.

As secretary of the freshman class, Eileen was eager to boost her class in any way she could and was recognized for selling the most tickets for the Freshman Harvest Festival project. She was also a member of Phi Sigma Kappa and IWC science club.

(Article written by Kay Freeland and Margaret Hickey)

MOM

*F*rances Meron Wilson came into this world at 2:30 pm, on December 18, 1910, (which happened to be on a Sunday) in Dallas, Texas. She was the daughter of Marie Elizabeth O'Brien Wilson and Homer T. Wilson. She was baptized January 22, 1911, at the old St. Patrick Church in Dallas. Rev. James Molloy officiated at this Sacrament of Baptism. Uncle Monk O'Brien and Aunt Ella O'Brien Vogel were the Godparents.

BABY FRANCES – 1911

The Sacrament of Confirmation was conferred on her at Sacred Heart Cathedral. She graduated from Ursuline Academy in Dallas in 1928, and attended Incarnate Word College in San Antonio, Texas.

As I have already mentioned, she married James Horace McCaffrey, November 28, 1929, at a Solemn Mass at Sacred Heart Cathedral.

I would like to interject here to bring you the "Nostalgia News Report" for the year of my mother's birth, 1910:

WORLD NEWS:	World's fair opens in Brussels, Belgium.
	Britain's King Edward VII died at age 68.
	South African Parliament holds first session.
NATIONAL NEWS:	Boy Scouts of America founded.
	New dance called the Tango is catching on in U.S.
	X-Rays proving useful in detecting lung disease.
	Mark Train's death mourned in the U.S.
	Talking pictures, Edison's latest invention unveiled.
MUSIC:	Ah! Sweet Mystery of Life
	Down By the Old Mill Stream
	Italian Street Song
	Mother Machree
	Naughty Marietta
SPORT NEWS:	Baseball World Series – Philadelphia Athletics
	Boston Marathon – Fred Cameron 2 hrs 28 min 52 sec
	U.S. Open Golf – Alex Smith

PRICES:	Regal 30 motor car – $1250
	Embroidered blouse – .98
	Victor Victrola – $125
	Solid Oak Bookcase without door
	– $1.00/section
	Average Income – $1,156.00
	New House – $3,395.00
	Loaf of bread – .04
	Gallon of milk – .34
	Gold per ounce – $20.67
	Silver per ounce – .54
	Dow Jones average – 82
INVENTIONS:	Electric Mixer, Bathroom Scales,
	Auto Transmission
PRESIDENT:	William Taft
VICE PRESIDENT:	James Sherman
LIFE EXPECTANCY:	50 YEARS

My mother studied music, the piano, from the first grade clear up into her college days. She played the classics beautifully. She is listed on her graduation program at Ursuline to play several pieces; "A Cottage Small" by Hanley, "Ave Maria" by Schubert, "Seguedillas" by Albeniz, and "Chromatique Galop" by Liszt.

I have a copy of her last Will and Testament from her senior year at Ursuline Academy.

Frances

Admirer of: Terrill and its contents (boy's school)

Noted for: Her voice

Wants to be: A nurse

Is: Red headed

Likely to be: a housewife

There is another list of sorts about her and her classmates. The title is "Can You Imagine? Frances being a turnover by others". At the bottom are the words, neither can we!

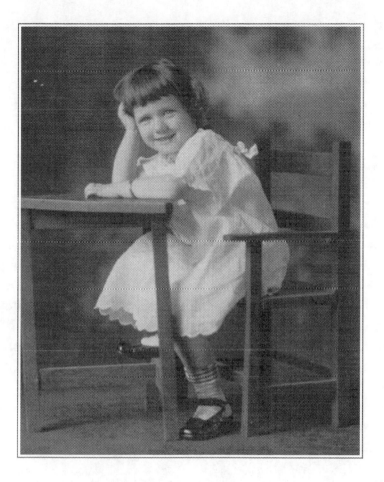

FRANCES – AGE 6

She had auburn red hair, and lots of it, and sparkly, blue eyes. My grandmother told us mom was a petite, lively little girl, very involved in her school activities. Grandma sewed many of her dresses on the old Singer sewing machine with the foot pedal. I still have some of grandma's old buttons.

I have a picture of my mom at age six, with the sweetest smile, wearing a white pique dress, scalloped around the hem. She had on knee socks, and black, patent leather Mary Jane shoes. I noticed she was wearing a gold bracelet. My grandpa owned a combination jewelry store and watch repair shop.

Mom was what you would call petite, barely five feet tall. In her later years, she seemed to have shrunk to four feet, eleven inches.

She maintained a gracious attitude with her beautiful smile. I sure don't remember many outbursts of anger or discontent. She never complained. She always welcomed my friends. I helped her a lot with the little ones and she always thanked me.

She kept a bottle of Bufferin in the kitchen cabinet, and took only one for whatever ailed her.

Mom told us about a certain happening. She had a devotion to Blessed Martin De Porres. Once she had a physical problem. She made a Novena, nine days of prayer, to Blessed Martin seeking his intercession with God. On the last day of the Novena, there was a knock at the door. A poor, black lady was there and asked if she could use the rest room. Of course, mom showed her to the bathroom. Then, the lady asked mom if she had any jewelry. Mom only had a couple pairs of ear rings, and offered them to the lady, hoping she could use them. The lady refused, and said good bye. As she walked out the door, mom went right after her to see if she could help in another way, but the lady had just vanished. My mother's physical problem ceased that very day. I have since learned that St Martin De Porres possessed gifts of healing.

I'll just be relating different situations about my mother. Here I am relating my memories. I saw a saying on a headstone at some cemetery: *"Memory is a golden chain that binds until we meet again."*

I was in the eighth grade, and it was Summer time, so all of us kids were home. A lady came to the front door, knocked, and introduced herself as representing some organization like Planned Parenthood. Mom was back in the kitchen and I told her about this visitor. She told me to go and round up all the children so this lady could meet us. We all gathered around. I watched my gracious mother. She had the baby in her lap and one of the toddlers at her side. So we each walked up as mom introduced us, shook the lady's hand and said, "How do you do mam". After all the introductions, my mother asked, "Now what is it you wish to speak to me about?" Do you know, that lady got up and left without a word?

It was customary for our good friends, Ted and Marie Saunders, to bring by a thanksgiving turkey. This particular time, someone else had also given us one. When Ted arrived with the turkey, one of the kids told him we already had a turkey. Ted told my mom to fix his turkey, and cook up the other one some other time.

Mom wrote about the fact that there were times when she and dad surely disagreed about something. After all, she would say, they both had Irish tempers. If she thought she was right about something, she would hold her point. Well, dad would do the same. Mom said she learned early on that if one of them was angry about something, the other should remain calm.

She told us once she was so angry with dad that she marched out of the house, and walked and walked, until she calmed down. Dad never said anything to her. She had completely gotten over her anger.

Mom told us about the time dad got the angriest as when she charged some things to their account. Dad asked her not to do this again. At first, she thought he was unreasonable, but later she knew he was right. She said the person trying to meet his obligations cannot do so with surprise bills coming in.

Mom told us that there were times when she became discouraged. She would call Aunt Dorothy for encouragement and wondered what Uncle Albert was thinking, what on earth did she need this time? They were always there for her. She said that when dad got discouraged, he became quiet, and would stay home a day to rest. This reminds me again, of those times dad checked himself into that hotel around the corner.

Our mother was gentle, kind and loving. She quietly went about her household duties. Seems to me she was the strength behind our dad, encouraging him onward and upward. She told us early on she knew she would have to share him with his fellowman. What a big heart she had. I mentioned before, that I was her number one helper, and oh, my goodness, how I watched her, always with such respect and awe. She was always in the present moment with God's Grace.

When dad had clients over in the evening, mom would very graciously excuse herself. She would say, "Please excuse me, I have children to care for in the morning." She would smile, and all was well.

One day, Sister Mary Angela walked to our house after school to talk to mom about Skip. Sister told me later, that after meeting our mother and all her children, she didn't have the heart to proceed with her problem. She just kept the visit to a nice social outing. My mother had enough to do. She would handle this boy on her own.

I can remember mom kept this big box in the hall closet. It was plum full of clothes to be ironed. We just reached in and pulled out what we needed to wear. I used to dream of the day when we could hire an official master of the art of ironing. In fact, after I helped get the little ones dressed and ready for school, I just pressed the front of my own Ship & Shore white blouse. I wore a sweater over it to cover the wrinkled back.

I loved our Catechism lessons with our mother. She sat calmly, and with such love in her heart, and would explain the truths of our Catholic faith taken right from the Bible. She showed us by her example, how much she loved Jesus and His Blessed Mother. The Great Commandment to love God with your whole heart, mind and soul, and to love your neighbor as yourself, came flowing out of her life. I learned what is meant by the present precious moment from her.

Since I am thinking about our mother, I will continue on and relate more of her life up until she joined our dad in heaven.

Mom wrote some of her thoughts down after dad died. She wrote that there seemed to be a fountain of giving at that time, Masses, flowers, cards, telegrams, and the clutch of many friendly hands. She felt she couldn't adequately thank everyone. The faith that our many friends and relatives had in her really sustained her.

Mom wrote, "What do you say of a man who had such convictions about his faith, and lived up to them, but that he was one of God's noblemen". She told us that it was dad's yearning to study and write in his golden years, but, as we know time ran out before he could fulfill this ambition.

Several years later, mom said she could not have made it without the people surrounding her and the strength God gave her. She continued to be involved with each child and their hopes and dreams.

As families grow, it wasn't long when the grandchildren came to be. Each child was special just like we were. Mom was over whelmed with gratitude and love as the years passed by. She would sit and express her joy and gratitude many times. This just made my heart soar. Then I too raised my mind and heart to the God who created me.

She was looking forward to growing old, surrounded by all our love and devotion. "How rich I am," she would say. However, there is much to be done, people to do things for, the sick to be visited, the elderly to be cheered, the bereaved to be comforted, for as she said, we must account to the Lord for our time. Are we doing all we can for Him, who has done so much for us? All the glory and honor belongs to God in everything I do, and I ask His guidance all the time. Wow!

I found an article which appeared in the Texas Catholic written by Debbie Landregan based on the "diary" Mom wrote shortly after Dad's death. I have already quoted from this diary but will fill in with some of Mom's comments:

LIFE NEVER DULL FOR MOTHER OF 17

The bright July sun trickled through the white sheers in Frances McCaffrey's living room as she settled into her favorite chair and began leafing through a small pile of typed and hand-written pages of paper that rested on her lap. The pages form Frances' diary, dedicated to her husband Jim but written for her children and their offspring.

Frances began the diary in 1960, a few months after her husband of 31 years, James and three of their children were killed in a car accident in West Texas that left two other children in serious condition.

"Death was probably so much on my mind at that time," Frances recalled of her decision to begin the diary. "I wanted to put down what was in my heart for the children to read. I wanted the children to know about their father and our relationship....the farther I got into it; the more I got into Jim and what he did."

Frances McCaffrey's story is interwoven with that of her husband's and those of her children- all 17 of them. As she read the words of her diary aloud, an image emerged of a loving relationship between man and wife and between the couple and their God.

There was something different about their dates while at college in San Antonio. Jim told her that he loved her on their third date. Their romance blossomed. The frivolity of our Dad proposing under that certain tree in Brackenridge Park was typical of the serious-looking man who would soon become her husband. "He had more nerve," Frances added with a hearty laugh.

Both Jim and Frances had once considered the religious life, Frances said. Her contact with a choral group of small children led Frances to think about serving as a sister. She said she later realized the Lord did have a vocation for her, not as a sister working with children, but as a mother of many children.

Later on after her marriage Mom said that it was in Evansville that Jim's pattern of helping others first emerged. "Never did I hear him turn anyone away who asked for his assistance, financial or spiritual."

The McCaffrey clan grew by leaps and bounds after settling in Dallas. Jim reached the top in both his work and in his faith. He was involved in many facets of Catholic life in the city.

Frances recalled a conversation she had with her husband just prior to the wedding of her daughter Angela. We were resting and he said, "Mother, if anything would happen to me, would you raise our boys and girls to be good men and women?" That conversation was the first thing that came when Frances was told of Jim and her children's deaths later that month.

I asked God why you didn't take me with them. Frances said. And then she recalled her earlier conversation with Jim. I knew I was going to have raise the rest of the children.

"At their deaths, I felt a cleansing myself, don't ask me why," Frances continued. "It was natural to have the company of his children to go along with him," she added of her husband's death.

Since the tragedy, Frances's time has been spent raising her family and continuing in the tradition of service to others and to the Church set by her husband. She is active in the Dallas Diocesan Vocation Guild (of which Frances served as president), the St. Monica altar society, and a member of the Ursuline Alumnae Association and is very involved in St. Monica's Legion of Mary which has spanned nearly 20 years. Frances said, "It takes hold of you."

Frances looks much younger than her age – 74 and describes herself as a "weeper," one who cries on both happy and sad occasions, and a rebel. "I don't look like a rebel but I am she noted with a chuckle.

Frances says she is constantly amazed by the love God has for her and her family. She jokes about the Lord coming through for her "at the last possible moment."

"All the glory and honor belong to God in everything I do and I ask his guidance all the time."

"I'm not a writer," Frances continued. "I was writing from my heart and once you do that, the words just flow out."

I remember mom was nearing 75. Her prayer to God was to please let her live to raise her children. That she did. Then, she looked at me and said, "You know, I would love to live till I'm 80. When she reached 83, she said that God was giving her some bonus years!

Our sister, Margaret Ann, had a beautiful talent for poetry.

Here are a couple of her poems. This one is to our mother.

MOM

Now that you don't need surgery and are out of bed,
Remember what the good doctor said.
Get on the streets and walk your mile,
It's a lot easier when done with a smile.
Your body has many useful muscles,
So strengthen them up, get outside and hustle.
Watch your calories and you'll get thin,
We'll be so proud of you – we'll all have a grin.
We love you so much – you're one great lady,
So show us how healthy you're going to be.

Here is another lovely poem written by Margaret Ann:

TO GOD

Oh Lord in the heavens up above,
You give us so much soothing love.
Be we rich or be we poor,
You always leave open your heavenly door.
Sometime my problems cause extra weight,
But I talk to you and they are gone – that is not fate.
Your compassion is great and you always forgive,
I will love you and serve you as long as I live.

From Margaret

P.S.
Thank you good Lord for my sweet mother, such a great mother like no other. Your Mother is no. 1 in the sky so blue, but my dear mother Frances is no. 2.

The following is a talk given by our mother to the 8th grade girls at St Monica's Grade School:

CHRISTIAN VOCATIONS
By Frances McCaffrey

I am here today as a Theresian to speak to you on Christian vocations. What, or who are the Theresians ? We are a group of ladies (like me) who closely associate ourselves with the Sisters. We feel that if Catholic womanhood can unite together in giving witness to its Church, the need to follow Christ is fulfilled. We are dedicated to a deeper appreciation of the vocation of the Christian woman, whether in the religious life, the home or in the office. And, we pray daily for over more than 750 different religious orders and for the Christian woman.

All of us mothers, daughters, sisters, nurses, and secretaries must unite and work together in doing what Christ wants us to do.

We used to think that a Christian vocation meant going into the religious life. Now, we think of the Christian vocation as that chosen by some as marriage, some to the celibate state of life in the world, others in formal dedication in the religious life.

What is the best vocation for you? The best vocation for you is the one to which you are dedicated – the one you want!

Your vocation today is that of a student – the best you can be! The Africans have a saying, "I will do my possible". Are you doing your possible?

Just as we can see our growth in a physical way year by year, so too, should we grow in mental and spiritual maturity.

You could say, "Who am I"? I would say to that question – I am Mrs. McCaffrey, mother of 17 children, that I love being a mother and consider it a privilege to be one, that I am a person who has feelings – I give a part of myself to others by loving and communicating with my children, friends and neighbors. You know the song, "I've Gotta Be Me". Each of us has something to give of ourselves that is unique and just plain "me".

In giving of ourselves, we are doing what is pleasing to God, and when we please God, we become a more Christian person.

We all need each other. The song, "People Who Need People Are the Luckiest People in the World", is true. How fortunate are each of you? Are you reaching out to help others (a smile for an elderly person, a pat on the back for someone who seems lonely, an encouraging word to one who needs it)? All of these are the "little ways" spoken of by the Little Flower, St. Therese. She showed us many countless ways to love God.

This is a wonderful age in which to be living (Sending a man to the moon, heart transplants, and much medical and technological advancement) and we should all want to meet its challenge. So, reach out to help others – help Sister with her many tasks, mother when she is tired, a friend with her math, and don't forget to let dad know how wonderful he is too.

Can you think of any way you can be of service to the Church in your own age group? Isn't it important that the Christian knows what she wants to do with her future? Next year, as freshmen, some of you will join us in the high school unit. Our high school units have been an inspiration. Young people have an important influence in modern society. Youth with its enthusiasm, sincerity and a certain idealism is greatly needed in the Church. We feel that these girls who are Theresians in their formative years can carry the movement into adulthood, the business world, and into their future homes.

In closing, I want to thank you for asking me to speak to you today and remember – "Without God, we cannot. Without us God will not."

I will continue the story as it unfolded after our dad's accident.

My sister and brother, Margaret Ann and Phillip, returned home from Pecos Hospital. After the car accident, they required ongoing care. Mom was hands on with them. Margaret Ann told me though, that for awhile, our mom would be back in her bedroom, sitting in her high back chair, in between her usual duties around the house.

While my mother was in Pecos, Texas, with Margaret and Phillip, someone took all the pictures of Dad, Eileen, Tom and

Steve, and placed them in a storage closet located in the corner of the girl's bedroom. One day Margaret made her way upstairs and found all those pictures. She called our mother, who just literally lit up upon seeing them. This was a turning- point in mother's recovery. It was a re-awakening. Mom placed those pictures around the house.

Margaret told me that everything happens for a reason. It was perfect timing for her to find those pictures. She and Phillip had healed well, and did not need mom's care as much.

Mom relates in her diary that she seemed to have come to life. She became involved with the Legion of Mary. She said the Legion was the focal point of her life, aside from her family. She was constantly surprised at God's graces which He imparts in such abundance. She wrote that because she was aware of her failings, she can only thank God all the day long.

She relates that some of her children were present for Mother's Day, May 8, 1983. Mom was 73. What a pleasant day it was. She lined everybody's cards up on the mantle, graced by the Sacred Heart picture. Best of all, that day was her family attending the Holy Mass with her. She always looked forward to receiving greeting cards of the season and the feast days.

Mom said she read several pages of her diary to the children, and they received joy and hope from them. She said, "think again how blessed we all are in His Grace."

I just remembered that our Mother loved those "Dear God" greetings by Annie. She saved some of her favorites. I will relate several of them now.

1. Dear God, life is wonderful when you have time to let it be. (2 kids sitting on a park bench).
2. Dear God, we couldn't do it without you...how come you didn't get a mention?
   (2 kids looking at a school program)
3. Dear God, admit it....there's just no end to all this learning.... (Little girl sitting at her desk)
4. Dear God, we use what we've got, and what we haven't got sometimes... (2 girls singing, one off key)

GRANDMOTHER FRANCES WITH 12 OF HER 29 GRANDCHILDREN

Mother Angelica of EWTN said the following, "We use the talents we possess to the best of our ability, and leave the results to God. We are at peace in the knowledge that He is pleased with our efforts, and that His providence will take care of the fruit of these efforts." This reminds me so much of our own mother. She would talk to us about the Providence of God. Many times a solution came forward at the last minute.

I will continue to write about our mother up until her passing on to Heaven. I was very involved in her care those last seven years or so, from 1987 to 1994.

After her children were raised, mom got busy serving her fellow man. She joined the Legion of Mary, the Altar Society, the Theresians, and she loved her Bible Study Group. She told me she would sit out on the patio in prayer, asking, "Now what, Lord? What do you want me to do now?" You just know that her spirit rested in the stillness of her being. There was a dialog going on between herself and her Holy Spirit. I just love the phrase, "Be still and know that I am your God." (Ps 46:10) It was at these moments that she got her marching orders.

Thanksgiving through the years, was soooo special, as all our families descended on 10520 Gooding Drive, Dallas, Texas. The hours of laughter and discussions were priceless. There we were, surrounding our mother, spread out all over the floor, as the available chairs were taken. I'm sure the grand children got a big kick out of hearing about the shenanigans of their parents. Christmas was to be spent at our own homes, with our families.

One of her granddaughters, Kelly, told me how much they loved their grandmother. Mom used to say, "Well, bless your heart," when her grandchildren were sharing with her. She was listening real well and would nod her head with a "yes, yes" from time to time, to indicate she was really present to them.

Mom carried on Grandmother O'Brien's tradition, when she sent gifts to her grandchildren, she included a holy card. Later I'll list the 29 grandchildren and now 45 great grandchildren with 1 more on the way, Sean and Jennifer's little one.

It was Easter Sunday of 1987; Margaret Ann called me to come over to her house. Mom was there and was not speaking clearly. Our mother was 77. By the time I got there, she appeared to be ok. This was the beginning of little "TIAS", transient ischemic attacks, which progressed to several strokes.

I asked mom to describe what happened when she had a "TIA", and she said she felt a sudden pain in her head, and then sort of slumped down. In fact, once I took her out to lunch at El Chico's, and on the way home she had a "TIA." It wasn't long until she recovered but it left her feeling weak.

Now, I am going to mention here, for all the future families, the importance of having the carotid arteries checked as we get older. The modern treatment for a blocked artery is very effective, and prevents strokes. Of course, keeping tabs on our cholesterol and triglycerides is important also. You see, this treatment was not available when our mother needed it.

From this time on, I kept a close watch on our mother, either by phone or actually dropping by to see her.

Sure enough, several months later, I was at work and got

a call from my brother Don, that mom had slumped down in her chair and could not move. There was a medical supply store nearby and I stopped by to pick up a walker and a portable potty chair for her. She had a stroke, and her speech was affected.

Her doctor determined that she could be cared for at home. He ordered Physical Therapy and Speech Therapy.

I was able to be with her for several days when my sister, Angela, came from San Antonio. Our little Mother recovered slowly but surely.

I explained to our mother what was happening. I told her that God had a new job for her. She looked at me with those big blue eyes, Oh, what? Well mom, you get to listen. You know people love it when someone is present with them and is listening. You have the ability to comprehend what is going on around you, and that remains a blessing. She nodded her head and smiled. Another thing I mentioned was for her to continue making her sounds. It just so happened that I was able to decipher her garbled speech. She used her fingers to indicate which of her children she wanted to talk about.

She worked real hard during the week, practicing the word sounds, taking the week end off. That is when some of her children and grandchildren would pop in for a visit. Sure enough, she regained about 80% of her speech.

We planned a surprise for the family. Mom relearned to say the Our Father. One weekend, we invited as many of the family as could come. We were all gathered and she stood up and prayed the Our Father. It was a most joyous happening.

In time, as the Lord would have it, mom had another stroke, along the same speech pathway in the brain. So there went her speech again, this time for good.

She did continue to make sounds. Sometimes she got frustrated trying to express herself. I taught her to stop trying, rest a little, take some deep breaths, and we would try again later on. This seemed to work.

One afternoon, I stopped by after her nap. When I walked

into her room, there she was, pointing her finger up to God. She was not happy, and she said "enough." (You see, she was able to say isolated words sometimes. In fact when we would sing around her she could sing along with us. Go figure.) So, I hopped onto her bed and she motioned for me to get my finger up too. I did. I said, "Lord, my mother has just about had it with all these strokes, could you give her a break?" Then she raised her arms up and praised the Lord. She motioned for me to do the same. I was so touched. I'm sure the Lord was too. I don't believe she had any more attacks after that day.

Soon, we hired agency nurses to help care for our mother during the day. I would relieve them after my usual work day. It wasn't long when I was getting very tired as Mom was up several times during the night. To give me some rest, some of my sisters , Joanne, Angela and Margaret, rotated weekends to care for her. I so appreciated their help. Margaret Ann helped me manage her care for awhile.

After some time, I became aware of two things. First, the cost of this care was eating away at mom's trust fund. Second, I saw that she had no company, no stimulation. The nurses would get her up and park her by the big bay window in the kitchen. I thought it was time for nursing home care, so I prayed about this.

One weekend I dropped by to see her and noticed she looked withdrawn and sad. So I remember standing in her kitchen by that big window and said, "Is it time Lord?" Do you know I felt a surge of electricity go through my entire body from my head down to my toes. I had clarity of vision on what to do next and an increase in physical strength.

I called Austin, Texas, to the nursing home agency, inquiring about the status of care at Heritage Manor located across the street from Plano General Hospital. This facility had one of the highest ratings in the state. I had heard about the good care provided and also about the waiting list to get in.

The next day I stopped by to see the Administrator. Do you have a bed for our mother? She hesitated and then said that one would be available in two weeks. Well, I just sat there a minute, and felt such relief. (Thank you Lord!) I told her that I would need to contact the rest of the family. Before I left, she showed me around and gave me this little book, "When Love Gets Tough; The Nursing Home Decision", by Doug Manning. I promised to have a decision in the next day or two.

I went right home and called the publisher of that book, and ordered nine copies, ASAP. I knew it might help us all to understand why this was going to be good for our mother. After many calls to my brothers and sisters, it was decided by the majority of us to place our mother in this home.

Two weeks rolled by. Several days before, I released the nurses. Angela came and we began preparing our mother for the change. Up front she knew she would become a neighbor of mine, since I lived a mile or so from the Nursing Home. Gradually, we rolled her wheelchair to different parts of the house, so she could choose which pictures etc. she wanted to take with her. Her favorite chair and end table would be included. We opened her closet and showed her dresses. She chose her favorite ones.

It was the night before we were to transfer her to her new home. She was giving me that certain look, like is this for real? So I asked Angela if she could put mom to bed. Angela told me that after mom was all tucked in, she took some Holy Water and blessed her. Our mother took a deep breath, closed her eyes and went off to sleep so peacefully.

The next morning, early, I heard her calling. I opened her door and she said, "Let's go"! Oh, I said, how about some breakfast first? We fixed her favorite oatmeal, toast, and coffee in her favorite cup. Angela and I hopped up on her bed and joined her. It was a most delightful breakfast. We got mom all dressed but it was still too early to make the journey up Coit Road. So Angela took her out to the back yard one last time. I finished packing her things. Ok, it's time to go mom.

Angela drove her and I went in my own car. She told me that mom started sliding down into the seat. She asked her if she was scared. Mom nodded and Angela told her she was too. This was going to be an adventure for all of us.

We pulled up to the Nursing Home. The Administrator must have seen us and met us at the front door. What does our little mother do? Well, she opened her arms to greet her and smiled at each one as she was welcomed. It was beautiful.

Angela and I stayed on to get our mother moved in. Indeed, there was activity going on all over the place. Angela stayed on several more days to ease the transition. The whole process was going quite smoothly. There is a saying by Socrates, "Sometimes one must wait till the evening to see how great the day has been."

After a week or so, mom was adjusting to the routine. Already I noticed a lightness in her spirit. She was taught how to get herself in and out of her wheel chair. She was taught how to wheel herself around the place. She would roll into the kitchen to get an extra banana.

Every other Monday, at 1:00 pm, was "manicure" day. Mom always finished her lunch early and somehow managed to be first in line. Her hair was washed and set weekly. I bought her several bright flowered cotton dresses that were easy to get on and off.

I'm remembering another story about her manicure. JoAnne and her daughter Suzanne were visiting. They took mom out to lunch at Wyatt's Cafeteria. They were having a great time, when all of a sudden, mom looked at her watch and started exclaiming about something. They figured out she wanted to return to the Nursing Home. So, when they got there, she wasted no time in getting herself to the manicure station.

The weekends were special as she spent Saturday or Sunday with us. There seemed to be one family or another dropping in to visit. I taped any musicals, the Lawrence Welk Show or other entertaining movies. She loved Notre Dame football, the New York Yankees, and John McEnroe, who had that Irish spunk.

She was able to pray her Rosary every day in the little chapel. She attended Holy Mass once a week there also.

It wasn't long when mother acquired the nickname "Spring Chicken". She was all over the place. In the afternoon, she would park herself out on the front veranda and greeted everybody coming in or out.

Here is an article written by my sister, Angela:

I REMEMBER MAMA
Frances Wilson McCaffrey

A LOVING, IRISH MOTHER
By Angela McCaffrey Notzon

The morning came all too quickly for both of us, Mom. I realized this was going to be the last time I'd fix your breakfast for you and care for you in your own home.

The decision to place you in a nursing home, after your stroke and continuing health problems, had come to reality. This was the day that we children were to relinquish our responsibilities to a more qualified staff of Nurses and professionals. My own feelings were that I had to be the "Mom" and go through with this decision that would affect your life, hopefully to improve your health in such a way that you would once again be cheerful and enjoy yourself and the people around you. I was looking to prolong your life so that, hopefully, you would regain your independence.

As I looked into your eyes that morning, I remembered your phrase, "This will hurt me more than you!" Now that the roles were reversed, I was finding out that "turnabout is not fair play."

I had come to you so many times seeking advice, consolation and love, and always received these things and the extra boost of your Irish wit. You always turned things around, and life was once again made right.

Mom, you and Dad taught us to go to our Heavenly Mother for help, and that is exactly what I did. At my early morning Holy Hour, I knelt down in front of Our Mother's altar and asked for assistance in seeing to the wellbeing of you, my Mom. After so many months of praying and continuing to care for you, the decision was truly an answer to those prayers.

You have been in your new home for over a month, and the nursing staff tells me that you are bringing joy and love and friendly greetings to all you meet. I even saw you pat someone on the arm as we were going down the hallway. I do believe you have found yourself a new ministry in your life. People again enjoy you and you are once more the "Mom" we all love.

That's my Mom! that little loving Irish woman, a joy for all to meet. You have been a unique mother to all your 17 children. It looks as though you are still a strong, independent soul sharing all of the talents God gave you.

I love you, Mom. Thank you for your loving and joyful example of Christian motherhood. You are still teaching me in your silent way how I am to live my life.

Another article written soon after her admission to Heritage Manor:

Frances Wilson McCaffrey

CONTINUING THE JOURNEY
By Maura Ciarrocchi

This is the ultimate nursing home success story. The heroine is Frances Wilson McCaffrey. She's 79.

Soon after taking up residence in the nursing home, Frances was honored with the title Ambassadress of the Heritage Manor Nursing Home in Plano, Texas. A series of strokes have affected her speech, but after adjusting to her new surroundings, she began to sit in the entrance hall and greet visitors and newcomers with a warm, friendly welcome. She became known as "Little Ballerina" because of the grace and dexterity with which she moved around the hallways in her wheelchair.

Her smile and cheerful spirit earned her the nick name "Spring Chicken." She gave no indication of the tragedies she had surmounted in her life.

The mother of 17 children, she overcame loss of two pregnancies the loss of two other children before they reached two years of age, the loss of her husband, daughter and two sons in a tragic automobile accident in which two of the children were seriously injured and, finally, the loss of her speech and mobility after several strokes.

A SURVIVOR

None of this defeated her. She felt the pain of each sad incident but continued looking on the bright side, living a principle she learned from her parents, that things happen for a reason and that negative events are opportunities to be accepted or changed.

Frances's daughter, Ursula, believes this is true of her mother's limited speaking abilities.

"Mom gets to listen, and people love to have someone to listen to them," she said.

In the past, she was active in a Dallas Vocation Guild, a life member of the Ursula Alumnae Association, a member of St. Monica's Legion of Mary and of a charismatic community, and past president of the Theresians in Dallas. She used the loss of those closest to her as a source of counseling others for many years in her parish, as always, sharing from her own experiences.

She wrote a story for her family because she "wanted the children to know about their father and our relationship." She and her husband, Jim, had a special relationship as husband and wife and as a couple with God.

A few years ago, when Frances' need for medical supervision became evident, her family was faced with a decision common in many families – whether or not to place their mother in a nursing home. It was a hard choice but obviously, for this family, the right one.

After the death of her husband and three children, Frances continued her journey with her remaining children. Her whole life has been – and still is – one of service to others.

Below is a tribute to our mother made at the Ursuline Academy Alumnae Homecoming events on May 6, 1989:

FRANCES WILSON MCCAFFREY AND CATIIERINE RICHARDSON HONORED AS THE 1989 URSULINE ACADEMY DISTINGUISHED ALUMNAE
By Kitty Cooper Wilson 73'

Frances Wilson McCaffrey, Class of 28' and Catherine Richardson, Class of 31' have been recognized as Ursuline Academy's Distinguished Alumnae for 1989.

Frances McCaffrey and Kate Richardson have exemplified the Christian ideals, standards and objectives of the Academy in both their public and private lives in an outstanding manner," according to Meriellen Lindeman Lehner, president of the Alumnae Association Board. "They truly live our school's motto,'Serviam' – to serve others."

The Distinguished Alumnae Award is an annual honor bestowed by the Alumnae Association upon Ursuline graduates. The award winners have distinguished themselves through personal and/or professional accomplishments and have rendered outstanding service to the community and Ursuline Academy of Dallas.

FRANCES MCCAFFREY, THE MOTHER

Frances Wilson McCaffrey has provided the definitive example for compellingly pursuing her vocation as mother of 17 children and devoted wife of Jim McCaffrey. Tragedy has played a major role in this large family, and Frances has faced her sorrows with humor, compassion, strength, love, determination and an unwavering faith in God. Her enthusiasm for living continues to sustain her family through their trials and serves as a primary source of inspiration.

"Mom set an example of dedication, hard work, love of God and His Mother and a willingness to help all those with whom she came in contact," according to Angela McCaffrey Notzon, class of 59', Frances' daughter.

Frances endured the loss of three children who died at birth or in infancy. A car accident took the life of husband, Jim and three more children. She managed to nurse the two children who survived the accident, but were left in critical condition, while consoling g her nine other children. In recent years, a series of strokes have diminished her health and impaired her speech. Earlier this year, she sustained another loss – the death of her son.

"Mrs. McCaffrey was a mother figure to me," according to Elizabeth Claudette Finegan, class of 53' and a friend of daughter Joanne McCaffrey Ameel, class of 54'. "After the tragic death of her beloved husband and three children, she was a woman of courage and fortitude, always calling on the name of the Lord."

Through her many losses and setbacks, Frances has maintained her belief that things happen for a reason and the negative events are opportunities to be accepted or changed.

Rearing her family left little time for outside work. But, once her children were grown, she became active and accepted leadership roles in various church-related activities. These have included the Teresians (now known as the Dallas Diocesan Vocations Guild), parish council of St Monica's Church and the charismatic movement.

Currently wheel-chair bound, Frances resides at Heritage Manor Nursing Home where her hospitality and welcoming presence to visitors have earned her the nickname "Little Goodwill Ambassador of Heritage Manor." She also is known as "Little Ballerina," for the grace with which she maneuvers her wheelchair through the home corridors, and "Spring Chicken," because of her sprightly demeanor. She is visited regularly by her children, grandchildren, great grandchildren and her many friends.

Now to continue our Mother's life at the nursing home. After supper, she would go around collecting little packs of bread, and then feed the birds out front. The Administrator, Bobbie, told me that when a difficult grandmother was admitted, she would call mom to come and sit with her. Our mother would pat her arm and soon calm prevailed.

I remember giving some instructions to the parents of all the families. Tell the grandchildren that from now on we only tell Grandma happy things. Also, keep the cards coming as she so enjoys them. When mom would pick out a certain finger that referred to which ever child was according to the birth order, I always quickly thought of something positive to tell her. For example, counting up to the 12th finger referred to her daughter Christine. She wanted to hear an update about Christine and so I would tell her what happy life events were going on at Christine's house. She was not to hear of any problems. We could discuss them among ourselves.

Marc Notzon, her first grandson, was getting married in San Antonio. "Would you like to go"? I Asked. Oh my goodness, she was so excited! Well off we went wheelchair and all. We flew on Southwest and stayed at Angela's house. Among the many pictures taken was one with our mother in the middle and all but one of her grandchildren present. I had that picture blown up to poster size at Walgreens and hung it on the wall beside her bed. She could be in bed and look at all those beautiful grand children. She would point to this child or that and I managed to give her a good report on each one.

I'll tell you a little more about her San Antonio trip. She handled the plane trip like a pro. Departing from Love Field, she was like a kid, pointing to the various structures below. She was taken to Sea World and enjoyed all the shows. When the trainers gave their hand signals to the whales, she gave hers also. She laughed when they seemingly obeyed her. She so loved feeling the porpoises.

Before returning, we took our mother over to the campus of Incarnate Word College where she met our father. Dubois Hall, where our mother lived as a student, was still there. I took pictures of it. In fact, her daughters, JoAnne, Angela and Eileen stayed in that same dorm. We cruised around Breckenridge Park and mom smiled as she recalled our dad's proposal to her under that certain tree.

It was her first Christmas in her new surroundings. We decorated a three foot tree, placing it on top of her table. December 18 was her 78th birthday. I invited the families to come on Sunday to celebrate. We took mom out to eat, and then met at our house for the birthday cake. She loved these get-togethers. There was always lots of laughter and reminiscing. The cousins got a chance to catch up with one another.

I made a note on June 6, 1992. By now mom was 82. Medicare covered another round of physical therapy as she had several falls. Her right knee would lock making it difficult to pivot in any direction. I dropped by mid-morning and she was just starting her physical exercise class. I mean to tell you she was really vigorous.

One weekend she was at our house watching the Rose Parade and she was just like a little kid, so excited to see everything. Next we planned to show her the Tony Awards that were previously taped. We have special video tapes marked just for "Grandma".

Remember I mentioned before about the present moment. She was always into it no matter what. She was loved by all. Her smile and twinkly blue eyes were her gift to everyone in return. She was truly present to whomever was in front of her at the time.

I mentioned that huge picture of the grandchildren, 20x30, on the sidewall beside her bed. Well, just below, were three more 8x10 pictures, her mother, father, and our dad. Many times I saw her reach over and tap, tap, tap on the glass covering her mother's picture, especially toward the end. "You'll see her soon," I said, and she smiled.

I was privileged to be with our mother for many hours especially during the final days and weeks of her earthly sojourn. There was an aura of peace surrounding her. I never noticed that she squeezed up her face. I can say that, several times, through the years of her care, I really cried a lot. I told God I really didn't want this job. (I was supported by my husband, Charles, my children Kirk and Colleen all during these years.)

You see, the mother becomes like the child, and I had to assume the mother role. I suffered from depression until the condition was treated. Boy, what a relief. It was on a certain Easter Sunday, Father gave his homily about the joy of the day. Man, I sat there thinking, you've got to be kidding. I didn't feel much joy. It was pure faith that helped me through this time. You see, these particular present moments were difficult ones. I just offered up each day to Jesus in spite of myself.

Several weeks before her passing, I thought this was it. She was on oxygen therapy and had periods of apnea. She would just not take the next breath for the longest. Then, she would rally. After the first few days of her last illness, sure enough, she rallied again. I remember kneeling down in front of her. She made this disappointing face and raised her arms up. She was ready to go home to Heaven. "Mama", I said, "God's plan is still working here. We need to remain present with Him." She nodded, smiled, and folded her hands in prayer. I just know that she was saying another "yes" to Him.

Now, I didn't know what the plan was, other than the present moment, so I went home that evening and called my brothers and sisters. "The Plan" unfolded as each of her children got to come and spend a quiet day with their mother. They got to share her meals and assist her. One child left this day, and another child came the next. This went on the rest of the week into the next.

She was tap, tap, tapping on her mother's picture again and then tapped on dad's picture. "Yes, mom, soon you will be with them", I said. She raised all her fingers, which meant she wanted to hear about all her children, even those who were already with Our Father in Heaven.

When her oldest son, Jim, arrived to be with her, she had just been admitted to the hospital. He was the last of her children to visit. On Friday, July 22, 1994, our mother was quietly taking one breath after another. Her doctor stepped into her room. He informed us that there was nothing more he could do for her. It was time for him to step aside and allow the Great

Physician, one more powerful than he, to take over. It was 5:00 pm. He told us he wanted to make our mother as comfortable as possible and to preserve her dignity.

After he left the room, I went over and quietly whispered in her ear, "Did you hear what he said?" She opened her eyes, pulled down her oxygen mask, turned her head to the side and winked. In other words, she had heard him. I was able to whisper some special messages to her and she nodded her head that she heard.

Within the hour, my son Kirk was there with her and her son Jim. Soon after Kirk left she took off her oxygen mask and had a beautiful smile as she looked up followed by several more breaths, and then she rested in peace. Our mother was 83 1/2 years old. I wonder who she saw when she looked up.

My sister, Angela, wrote the following tribute to our mother:

TRIBUTE

I think that all who knew Frances would confirm that this lady had a capacity to love everyone she met.

Mom was the "heart" of our family, the one who gave us our life's blood and sustained us through life's challenges. It was her strength of character and strong will that she passed on to her family through the virtue of love without limits. In her gracious and quiet way she raised all of us to never lose hope.

She lived her life in a way that was full of joy and by her example we have developed a spiritual way of life by loving our Creator and others. She made a difference in this life for all.

Mom's life made a great deal of sense and followed a perfect pattern. She was given this beautiful gift of love, and when the time came and all the children were raised, she naturally participated in plenty of projects that had her one required ingredient – love! Love she had. She gave her all to do the best job and always with such enthusiasm! From her early years through her school days to her married life with Jim and children, to her active service years, and through her nursing home experience, she shared her most valuable assets: her smile and her love.

Now, our Mom has attained her eternal reward and so we celebrate today. Thank you Lord, for all the benefits you have given us through "Frances".

Angela McCaffrey Notzon

Angela also wrote another tribute to our Mother.

FRANCES WILSON MCCAFFREY
PARALLELS TO
MOTHER TERESA OF CALCUTTA'S BUSINESS CARD

"THE FRUIT OF SILENCE IS – PRAYER"

Our Mom has been speechless for 8 years!! She has been in a world of sounds and verbal communication but not for her. She has been in a watchful state of seeing all around her and enjoying what she sees but not having the ability to add what she would like or to participate fully in a shared conversation. She has been left in the nursing home in her room where we say goodbye and the silence begins. I know now that the silence she was experiencing was "prayer".

"THE FRUIT OF PRAYER IS – FAITH"

Of course our Mom was in communication with her Creator. The peaceful expression on her face when we had to leave and as we turned out the door, it was evident. She was in God's hands. As she so often did, she raised her eyes up and had that beautiful smile and the message was He (the Lord) was there!! Always she gave us that confidence that she was in the hands of the Lord and that she was fine.

"THE FRUIT OF FAITH IS – LOVE"

I think that all who knew Frances would confirm that this lady had a capacity to love anyone she came in contact with. She loved all her babies all the way through, including the troublesome teens when we still received that beautiful smile that all was ok. I know that she must have known that God was blessing her with these children because of their love for one another (Mom and Dad's). She knew and felt God's love on all she did. That love continued when we all left home for she would reach out to so many others and give that encouraging smile and words of wisdom and help.

"THE FRUIT OF LOVE IS – SERVICE"

It's beginning to make sense and it's following a perfect pattern. Mom was given this beautiful gift to love and when the time came and all the children were raised, she became a natural to find plenty of projects to participate in that the one ingredient that was a must – love! That she had and was ready to give all she had to do the best job and always with such enthusiasm!!

"THE FRUIT OF SERVICE IS – PEACE"

With all the unbelievable wars and violence in the world, our Mom was able to keep a family going in a sound and beautiful home. Just the idea that there couldn't possibly be any confusion in a household as big as ours is an understatement at best. What was always there was a home to all who entered and lots of fun and excitement and love and caring to go with it.

What brings this all to an end is the eternal reward our Mother has attained as she is truly experiencing all the fruits of her labor.

Thank you Lord for the benefits you have given to us thru
FRANCES

This poem by Helen Rice captures our mother's spirit. It is like she is talking to us.

When I must leave you
For a little while,
Please go on bravely

With a gallant smile
And for my sake and in my name,
Live on and do all things the same –
Spend not your life in empty days,
But fill each waking hour
In useful ways –
Reach out your hand
In comfort and in cheer,
And I in turn will comfort you
And hold you near.

Helen Steiner Rice

Here are comments made by our cousin, Rev. Carl Vogel, at our mother's funeral. There were present: five sons, 5 daughters, 29 grandchildren, 23 great grandchildren, and one sister, Lillian Reed.

Frances McCaffrey 30 July, 1994

A gracious lady passed from this earth to the realm of Heaven. It is our sorrowful duty and yet a loving privilege to speak at the funeral service of one with such a magnificent character.

Sentiments of sympathy are found on our lips because we know a family has lost their guiding light, their mother, their grandmother, relative and friend. Sentiments of prayer are found in our hearts to whisper petition to the Almighty, that He, our loving God, will sustain you in bearing your cross of sorrow.

In the year of 1930, Sir Thomas Lipton, who made Yachting a famous international water sport, wrote his life biography. The very first paragraph expresses a feeling that fills our hearts this morning. He wrote a good start is half the battle. I don't know who originated that phrase, but I do know that nothing more true has been written in words. I had a good start, for I had a good mother. The best, the bravest-hearted, the noblest mother God ever sent from Heaven to be one of His angels on earth. I loved my mother dearly in life, and although she has been gone many years, I can honestly say that not a single day passes without some beautiful memory of my mother coming to me and sweetening the hour of her coming.

Whatever I am, whatever I possess, whatever I have done, is due to the little Irish lady from Clones, in Ulster. She was my guiding star, and by the light of that star, I shall steer for the time that remains to me.

What a beautiful expression of noble sentiment! What Sir Lipton said of his mother, you, Frances' children, can say the same? Whatever you are, whatever you have done, are due to your dear mother. She has been your guiding star in your life.

As stars led the seamen/mariners of old on a course to safety, if you guide your lives by the star of your mother then you will reach the haven of heaven.

Suppose you were asked to write Frances' biography, the story of her life. What an inspiring account it would make for all mothers young and old. Our biography would have to go back to her very childhood. It must have been a sweet, innocent childhood, because the foundation of all worthy characters is laid in those tender years before a child ever starts to school.

We could tell of her home, and the good mother she had. Good mothers train good mothers. Her years in school were obedient, cheerful, and even then she showed the spirit of un-selfishness that marked her entire life.

Her teens were innocent and happy years, with the growth of mind and body, her beautiful soul kept pace. An outstanding date during her college life was her meeting Jim McCaffrey, and later their wedding in 1929.

In her biography we note that she never attended a meeting of planned parent-hood or what have you. She listened and heeded the promptings of faith and reason and gladly accepted the children that God sent her. Otherwise, some or even all of you dear children would not be here today.

In her story we would write of those expectant days that became weeks and months of her prayerful gratitude to Almighty God, for it was always a time of sweet, beautiful hope.

Bright among the pages of her biography would be those that marked the birth of her first child, James Joseph. Because she had a faith, a deep strong Catholic faith, she realized as she held her first born, that God had chosen her as a co-creator with Him, in bringing that little one into the world. The birth of each of you children was a reliving of Jimmy's birth, for each of you it was a time of joy, a time of thanksgiving, a time of hope.

There would be one chapter speaking of her love and affection which she brought to her beloved husband for more than 31 years, as a loving wife, interested co-worker, sharing bad times and the good, in joy or sorrow. Truly, it must be said of her that above all creatures on earth, her husband came first and always.

Foremost too was her love for her children, whether in the field of play, the realm of learning, whether it be to nurse the hurts, or stand vigil over the bed of pain. Her children were precious gifts given to her by a loving God.

Other bright chapters we could spend in describing the mother on her way to church, kneeling before her God, approaching the Communion rail. Next, we would relate her unspeakable happiness as each one of you received your first Holy Communion, the Sacrament of Confirmation, and later, the Sacrament of Matrimony.

At least one chapter we would fill with examples of her kindness to friends and neighbors, of her beautiful gift of love for all.

There would be dark passages in that biography, the loss of her third child, a daughter, at the precious age of eighteen months. Then, the shocking death of her husband, and three of the children in a car wreck in West Texas.

Even the loss of her loved ones, the darkness would be sprinkled with the stars of her courage, her trust in God, and in her confidence of meeting them again.

Finally, we would have to record her stroke, which took away her gift of speech, yet, she remained ever pleasant and smiling. This cross she bore for six and one half years, offering up her suffering for you, her children, and her grand children.

Finally, we would have to record the last months and moments of her life, this funeral, your sorrow.

We spoke of the star that has helped guide you on the sea of life. By doing this, we cannot help but think of our Heavenly Mother, Mary. Mary has many titles, one that is "Star of The Sea." Your dear mother taught you to love your Heavenly Mother, so that Mary would also be your guiding star bringing you closer to her Son, Jesus.

Never, never, lose sight of those two stars Mary's and your mother's star. They are shining together in Heaven.

The following are various condolence messages from family and friends sent after our Mother left us:

August 1, 1994
Dear Friends,
We have never met. However, because of our relationship with Frances, I feel like we do know you a little.

July 31st, we returned from a short vacation and saw the obituary for Frances in the paper. We were saddened for her family and want you to know we are holding you in our prayers.

We met Frances at Heritage Manor Nursing Home on Coit Rd. Walter's mother, Grace Evans, was a resident there from October of 1998 until her death on March 3, 1991. We visited the home daily where most often Frances and her wonderful smile were at the front door greeting us. I visited with her often. Even though her speech was impaired, I could usually understand what she was trying to say. She told me about her large family and all the love and joy (and a little sadness, too) she had experienced. Later she made it known to me how frightened she was about having the cataract surgery and I tried to ease her concern the best I could. I would sometimes wheel her from place to place and I really developed a sincere love for her. She often invited me into her room where she shared various love gifts and pictures. After Grace died, we visited the home a few times and as usual were greeted by Frances at or near the front door.

110

Since the spring of 91', we have not returned to the Manor. We have many good memories there but also those which we choose to be separated from. We know Frances' last years were full of love from her devoted family. She was definitely one of the joys we encountered during a very difficult time in our lives. We praise God for her life and can only imagine the peace and love which she is now experiencing in her new life.

With deepest sympathy,
Marilyn and Walter Evans

From some of the Grandchildren:

To all my Aunts and Uncles,
Upon receiving the news of your Mother's and my Grandmother's passing, I first had a feeling of loss. Secondly, I thought, at last she is not suffering. Third, I thought, she is now in the house of the Lord. Fourth, she is now with your father, my grandfather, James H. McCaffrey. Her smile is forever "etched" in my heart. I am overwhelmed at the fact that I can truly say that Frances M. McCaffrey was my grandmother. God bless all who will feel her absence. I love you grandmother. And I love all of you.

With highest admiration and deepest sympathy,
James H. McCaffrey II
Bernarda A
James J McCaffrey II

Thinking of our Mother as we read the following poem:

Think of standing on a shore
And finding it Heaven!
Of taking hold of a hand
And finding it God's hand!
Of breathing a new air
And finding it celestial air!
Of feeling invigorated
And finding it – immortality!

Of passing from storm and tempest
To an unknown calm!
Of waking and finding –
I am home.

Phyllis McGinley

Now sit back and listen to Mom talking to us. (Author unknown)

TOGETHERNESS
Death is nothing at all – I have
Only slipped away into the next
Room. Whatever we were to each,
That we are still. Call me by
My old familiar name, speak to
Me in the easy way which you
Always used. Laugh as we
Always laughed at the little jokes
We enjoyed together.
Play, smile, think of me, pray for
Me. Let my name be the
Household word it always was..
Let it be spoken without effort.
Life means all that it ever meant.
It is the same as it ever was; there
Is absolutely unbroken continuity.
Why should I be out of your mind?
Because I am out of your sight?
I am but waiting for you, for an interval,
Somewhere very near just around the corner.
All is well.
Nothing is past; nothing is lost.
One brief moment and all will be
As it was before – only better,
Infinitely happier and forever we
Will be one together with Christ.

A note from her grandson, Christopher Thomas McCaffrey:

Dear Aunts, Uncles and Cousins,

I cannot find the words I feel now. I will always remember Grandma with that smile of hers and the way she always listened to us when we had something to say. I know she is up there with God and looking down on us and smiling.

Take care. My prayers are with you.

Your Nephew and Cousin,
Christopher Thomas McCaffrey

A letter from Jack W. Mackey:

To the family of Mrs. Frances McCaffrey,

I was a friend of your grandparents, Horace and Mary McCaffrey of Milwaukee, having visited them in their home when I was a young boy in the early 1930's.

My family and I were very good friends of your Harry and Elise McCaffrey. In fact, I always called her aunt Elise. I still visit their grave every Christmas eve at the old Oak Cliff Cemetery. I remember when she died on June 6, 1940 and Uncle Harry died in June 1969.

I know your dear mother is happy in being re-united with the beloved husband Jim and her children, Mary Elise, Dorothy, Don, Tom, Steve, Eileen and Charles Joseph...all in Heaven now.

It seems like only yesterday when you're Dad along with Steve, Tom, and Eileen were killed on Thursday August 25, 1960 near Pecos, Texas.

I remember Bishop Danglmayr said your Dad was a Christian with a deep since of practical religion. He was speaking of the personal charities that your Dad never talked about. I remember your Dad spent his own money and his talent to help people who needed a friend.

I remember your dear Mother wrote a newspaper article in the 1950's titled "What Christmas Means to Me"....she read it to me before she sent it to the Dallas Times Herald.

I also recall that it was the custom of Jim and Frances for the

McCaffrey family to recite the rosary each evening in the family living room.

I was in the insurance business like your Dad and I enjoyed going to luncheons in the old Southwestern Life Insurance building with your Dad and Mr. Jim Walsh, another lifelong friend.

I even remember meeting your uncles C.J. and Nute and your aunt Ruth when I was in Miwaukee in 1934, yes, 60 years ago!

In remembering your parents and grandparents, my mind started looking back to where and when it all began, in Dallas and Milwaukee in the 1930's. Seeing the McCaffreys and the Mackeys together in those days, then slowly leafing through the memories we all make together to bring us to where we are today.

A Roman Philosopher wrote:

"Life is a play, tis not it's length but its performance that counts".

To me, I'll say that your Mother's life was a full-length play and we all know that the performance was unforgettable!

Sincerely,

Jack Warner Mackey

A lovely note from our neighbor who lived on Bowser Ave, Ellen McRedmond:

Dear Angela, Joanne, Ursula and All McCaffreys,

So sorry to hear of the death of your precious Mother. I regret I couldn't be there with you and glad Tony and Jean could be there with you. She surely was 'the heart of your lives'. I remember so well what a happy person she was – so faith-filled. I know your Dad is glad to welcome her into Heaven and into his arms again and Eileen and all the rest of you already there. I wish I could be with each one of you. You are in my heart and prayers; I think of you every day since I found out about your Mother. I'm sure she is praying for you from her very special place with God.

Lovingly,

Ellen McRedmond

A letter from Jan Brunson who lived 2 doors down on Bowser Ave:

Dear Ursula,

Thank you for calling me about your Mother – I called Bettye Sue that morning at her office in Plano so she could get in touch with you.

I asked my Bible class at St Bernard's to add Frances's name to our prayer list. I think you know I joined the Catholic Church 12 years ago when I moved into my home here 2 blocks from St Bernard's. I had been in the Episcopal Church 40 years and I'm glad I finally joined the Catholic Faith I loved since childhood.

Your Mom and Dad, Jim, had something to do with my fondness for God's Catholic Church. I really enjoyed the times I came over to your front lawn on Bowser and sat and talked with your dad, Jim and Frances. Any subject you name it was ok with them, but best of all they accepted me just as I was, a growing-up teenager graduating from high school and beginning college at SMU. They were able to make me feel that what I felt or believed was important. My own parents were always too tired, too busy, or so I felt as a teenager. So, it was nice to feel like I made new adult friends in your parents.

That's how I remember both of them – sitting on the lawn chairs – your mother doing something with her hands, probably peeling something to eat, but easily comfortable talking to whoever wanted to visit with them.

We all sat outside no one had air conditioning – those were hot summers. How did we ever go through those days? We just did, that's all.

Thank you again for sharing with me that you're Mother was in Heaven. I was not going to be able to come at the time of the services. She has been on my mind all week long.

Love to you and your family,
Jan Brunson

THE JIM & FRACES MCCAFFREY FAMILY

LIVING MEMBERS
AS OF THIS DATE OCTOBER, 2008

JIM MCCAFFREY

CHRISTOPHER MCCAFFREY

JAMES H MCCAFFREY II
JAMES J MCCAFFREY II

RHONDA MCCARVILLE

PATRICK & JONA LEE MCCAFFREY

KELLY ANN MCC. SCHWOEBEL & PAUL SCHWOEBEL
CHRISTOPHER MONDRAGON & FELICIA
MONDRAGON
KERRI ANN MONDRAGON & ROBERT SABADO
AALIYAH SABADO
ROBERT SABADO

KATHLEEN MCC. & MARK BOWERS

JASON BOWERS & PATRICIA BOWERS
ALYSSA SISNEROS
JOHN BOWERS

COLLEEN MCC. JOOSTEN & WILLIAM JOOSTEN

116

ANTHONY JOOSTEN
STEPHEN JOOSTEN

EILEEN MCC. FALLIN & GARY FALLIN

BLAKE FALLIN
SEAN FALLIN

MAUREEN MCC. HENDRICK & DAVID HENDRICK

MICHAEL HENDRICK
MARK HENDRICK
RACHEL HENDRICK

ERIN MCC. SCHAEFFER & CHRIS SCHAEFER
MEGAN RODRIGUEZ
AMBER RODRIGUEZ
JOSHUA RODRIGUEZ

JOANNE MCC. AMEEL & JIM AMEEL

SUZANNE AMEEL LEGGETT
EMILY LEGGETT
RYAN LEGGETT
ANNIE ROSE LEGGETT

CHRISTOPHER AMEEL & LISA AMEEL
ALEXANDRIA AMEEL

ELIZABETH AMEEL MORROW & LUKE MORROW
ABIGAIL MORROW
LUKE MORROW

JOHN CHARLES (SKIP) MCC. & GENEVIEVE BOERNER
MCCAFFREY

SEAN MCCAFFREY & JENNIFER BROWN MCCAFFREY
ALONNA GABRIELLE MCCAFFREY
CONNOR MCCAFFREY
CHRISTIAN MCCAFFREY

LISA MCC. HICKERT & BRIAN HICKERT
RACHEL HICKERT
GUNTER HICKERT

URSULA MCC. HEUISER & CHARLES HEUISER

KIRK HEUISER & KAWAI LUCID HEUISER
AMBERLE HEUISER
BRIANNA HEUISER
CALEB HEUISER

COLLEEN HEUISER SCHMIDT & JEFF SCHMIDT

ANGELA MCC. NOTZON & AL NOTZON

MARC NOTZON & DENICE GROTHUES NOTZON
GARRETT NOTZON
ELISE NOTZON
ANNE NOTZON
AIDAN NOTZON

ROBERT NOTZON & MARYANNE IGUBAN NOTZON
PABLO NOTZON
MARIA NOTZON

EILEEN NOTZON LUNA & JOHN LUNA
TRAVIS LUNA
HARRISON DENN
TREVOR DENN
ISABELLA LUNA

BRIDGET NOTZON BROWN & DAN BROWN
ETHAN BROWN
DEVON BROWN
SAGE BROWN

ANNELISE NOTZON

MICHAEL MCCAFFREY

COLIN MCCAFFREY & CHARLENE LYLE MCCAFFREY

MARGARET MCC. COSBEY & BILL COSBEY

MICHAEL HOYT & LESLIE HOYT
MCKENZIE HOYT

DYLAN HOYT & MELANIE SAILER HOYT
MURPHY HOYT
MAGUIRE HOYT

CHRISTINE MCC. GRIFFIN & MICHAEL GRIFFIN
SCOTT GRIFFIN

MONICA GRIFFIN PATEL & DR. ANUT PATEL

AARON GRIFFIN

PHILIP MCCAFFREY

DECEASED FAMILY MEMBERS:
JIM MCCAFFREY – 10-6-09 8-25-60
FRANCES MCCAFFREY – 12-18-10 7-22-94
MARY ELISE MCCAFFREY – 1-18-34 6-28-35
CHARLES MCCAFFREY – 11-25-36 11-25-36
DOROTHY MCCAFFREY – 11-30-50 11-30-50
DONALD MCCAFFREY – 7-30-45 2-21-89

EILEEN MCCAFFREY – 6-1-41 8-25-60
STEVE MCCAFFREY – 8-18-46 8-25-60
THOMAS MCCAFFREY – 3-2-52 8-25-60
BRIAN AMEEL – 1-17-67 7-14-95
MARYANNE MCCAFFREY – 12-3-59 3-7-95
JERRY MCCAFFREY – 12-2-32 1-14-97
SHANNON MCCAFFREY – 6-13-69 1-22-72
JUDITH MCCAFFREY THOMAS – 1-5-39 3-23-97

DAD AND THE FOOD CHAIN

*M*ost of the time dad left the running of the house to mom. Occasionally, though, he would step up to the food plate and volunteer his services.

Recently, I was in Wal-Mart, here in Mountain Home, and I noticed a can of Ovaltine. I stopped, and just chuckled to myself. You see, one of my dad's business associates said to him one day, "Jim, there's a new drink out now with lots of vitamins. It's called Ovaltine. You would do well to get this for your kids – part of good nourishment." So, dad came home with some Ovaltine. He took on the task of making the first batch himself, in one of mom's largest pots. It looked to me as if he dumped a whole gallon of milk in there and practically emptied out the Ovaltine container. Meanwhile, us kids got our cups and lined up, littlest first. You know we liked it! That began the periodic consumption of a nutritious drink.

Another time we didn't fare as well. Once again, one of dad's business associates told him about all the wonderful nourishment in hominy, it's plum full of Vitamin B. Dad walked in that afternoon with a whole case of the stuff. That evening, at supper, mom heated up several cans and when we got settled around that twelve foot-long table, there, plopped on every plate, was this "nourishing Vitamin B hominy." After the blessing, dad proceeded to explain this new addition to our meal, and asked us to go for the big taste test. We did! I wish you could have seen the faces contorted this way and that. No one liked it. The rest of the food was distributed. We continued as always with our dinner with one exception, that "nourishing Vitamin B hominy", remained on every plate! Dad tried to explain that it was good for us, and he really wanted us all to finish what was on our plate. Well, we all just sat there. Dad said "no one leaves this table until your meal is finished." To us, our meal was finished; it just did not include that "nourishing Vitamin B hominy." Then, our mom said, "now Jim." That was the end of it! I really don't know what happened to the rest of those cans of hominy.

Dad loved pumpernickel bread and limburger cheese. I don't believe I ever tasted either one, but oh, how odiferous was the cheese!

I was again at the Wal-Mart store at the deli counter, looked down and noticed a loaf of pumpernickel bread. A warm feeling came over me as I remembered dad. I smiled, reached down, and bought a loaf. It really was delicious after all.

One evening, in high school, I had some friends over. Dad walked in, carrying a silver tray with a block of his limburger cheese, crackers, and a small knife neatly placed on top. He had a white towel hanging over one arm. Without saying a word, his head and nose up in the air, in a most proper butler pose, he went to each person, bent over, and offered the tray right under their nose. The first person said, "No thank you" and so on. He then calmly and properly left the room and returned to bed. We cracked up with laughter!

I will never forget the iced tea fiasco. It was a typical summer day in Dallas. Dad was always home for supper. This certain day, after the blessing, dad got our attention and explained that he was very tired, had a hard day at work. So, he wanted each of us to prepare our iced tea now, instead of throughout the meal. He did not want to hear the cling-clang of our spoons against our glasses. "OK, everybody put your sugar in your tea." We did. "Now, when I count to 3, everybody stir your tea, all at once. This is your last chance, stir good." I remember we all sat there, holding our spoons upright waiting for the final countdown. Depending on how you looked at it, the sound of all those spoons was piercing, or a type of melody.

Once dad brought home a bunch of live chickens and pinned

them to the clothes line upside down. Mom had a huge pot of boiling water to the side. After cutting off the head, dad handed each chicken to mom, who dipped it into the water, and then handed the chicken to us to de-feather. You see, my mom was a petite city girl. I watched her cut those chickens up. Her face was not the usual pleasant one that we saw on a daily basis. You can be sure, we never did this again.

Every now and then, mom would give dad the grocery list and he would shop. One day, she had 3 cans of Tomato soup on the list. He came home with a case. He said, "It's cheaper when you buy by bulk." The thing about buying a whole case was it would leave her less money for some other items.

One summer dad decided to plant some corn out back. We all helped to "plow" up the earth. It was a small patch of ground. Sure enough, those stalks of corn actually grew. Our neighborhood friends inspected the crop. I don't remember sharing any as we consumed it all. That was our last attempt at gardening.

Dad had some Italian friends, the Scotino's. Mrs. Scotino showed him how to make meatballs and tomato sauce. Once a week, he did the honors, and made this for us. To this day, we all love spaghetti and meat balls!

In the 1940's and thereafter, dad would take mom to Campisis. He knew Mr. Campisi and would always order the spaghetti with two meatballs. The menu used the plural "meatballs". One time, dad was served his spaghetti with one meatball. He called the waiter and asked for his other meatball. The waiter explained that now, spaghetti is served this way. Dad picked up the menu, and there it was, plain as day, "meatballs". He called for Mr.Campisi, who graciously came over. "You're going to have to change your menu if you intend to give me one meatball." And so, dad received his second meatball. The next time he dined at Campisis , the menu read "meatball". To this day, whenever any of us are in Dallas, we go to Campisis.

There were two other restaurants dad would take mom and sometimes us to: The Spanish Village, and Jay's Marine Grill. I do remember the hot rolls at Jay's. Dad would call home and tell mom to get ready, he was taking her out. It was always a surprise. We older ones would finish getting the supper on.

Dad and mom would go to early Mass during the week. Sometimes, they would stop off at the Carnation coffee shop on the corner of Oak Lawn and Lemon Avenue. I can't help but wonder at their discussions, so much to plan for.

REMEMBER WHEN?

For several years I have been jotting down little memories. It's really been fun. So, I have decided to "reminisce." I am just going to start and you may notice some rambling on and on.... Might as well start with 1938, the year of my birth:

HEADLINES: Hitler appoints himself as minister
President # 32 is Franklin Delano Roosevelt
Miss America is Marilyn Meseke (Ohio)
49 hour work week established in U.S.
Ball point pen invented
Howard Hughes flies around world in 3 3/4 days
Orson Wells "War of the Worlds" causes widespread panic
Ernest Hemingway publishes "The Fifth Column"
Sea Biscuit, that famous horse

FOOD PRICES: Bread (1 Lb) .09
Coffee (1lb) .23
Eggs, (doz) .36
Margarine (1lb) .18
Milk (½ gal) .25
Round steak (lb).35

HIT SONGS: A Tisket A Tasket
Falling In Love with Love
Flat Foot Floozies with a Floy, Floy
September Song

<pre>
                        You Must Have Been a Beautiful Baby
FILMS: Le Quai, Des Brumes
                        Pygmalion
                        The Lady Vanishes
</pre>

Best Actor: Spencer Tracy (Boy's Town)
Best Actress Bette David (Jezebel)
Best Picture You Can't Take It with You

PULITZERPRIZE:

Drama: Thornton Wilder (Our Town)
Fiction: John MarQuand (The Late George Apley)
Poetry: Marya Zaturenska (Cold Morning Sky)

NOBEL PRIZE:

Peace: Nansen International Office for Refugees
Physics: Enrico Fermi (United States)
Medicine: Corneille J.F. Heymans (Belgium)
Medicine: Richard Kuhn (Germany)

Deacon Richard wrote an article once asking the question, "What is a survivor?" The answer: "Anyone born before 1945."

Yep, we were born before television, penicillin, polio shots, frozen foods, Xerox, plastics, contract bonuses, Frisbees, and the pill.

We were born before radar, credit cards, split atoms, laser beams, ball point pens, pantyhose, dishwashers, clothes dryers, electric blankets, air conditioners, drip dry clothes, and before the man walked on the moon.

Bunnies were small rabbits, and rabbits were not Volkswagens. Having a meaningful relationship meant getting along with our cousins. We thought fast food was what you ate during Lent.

We were born before day-care, group therapy, and nursing homes. We never heard of fm radio, tape decks, electric typewriters, and it wasn't too long ago, I thought, "what in the world is www.com?" I wondered how in the world will I ever learn the "internet".

What about artificial hearts, word processors (I can still see the ink well holders on the corner of our school desks).

Time sharing meant togetherness. A chip meant a piece of wood, and hardware meant hardware, software wasn't even a word.

The term "making out" referred to how you did on your exam. Pizzas, McDonalds, and instant coffee were unheard of.

We hit the scene when there were actually 5 & 10 cent stores, where you bought things for 5 & 10 cents. I loved the Woolworth store. For one nickel you could buy an ice cream cone, ride a street car, make a phone call, buy a Pepsi, or Coke, or enough stamps to mail one letter and two postcards.

You could buy a Chevy or Ford for under $600, but who could afford one? A pity too because gas was only 11 cents a gallon!

Cigarette smoking was fashionable, grass was mowed, Coke was a soft drink, and pot was something you cooked in.

In the '40's there was a war going on. I have a book of those coupons mom used to purchase sugar, lard, and several other items. My brother Skip would go up to the back of the grocery store to see what came in that day. He would rush home to tell mom. I still remember that piece of lard. Some of our neighbors would give mom their leftover coupons. We took our red wagon through the neighborhood collecting donations of iron pieces for the war effort.

We had hardwood floors. I can still see that can of Johnson & Johnson wax, with that very greasy rag tucked inside. It was down on our knees time to wax those floors. ...and that wasn't the end of it. We had to buff and buff. (That was before electric buffers.)

Mom had a cleaning routine. We all had our assignments. On Saturday, we worked real hard to get everything done by 12:00 pm, and then we could go up to the Esquire, Delman or Village Theatre to see Roy Rogers and Dale Evans. A special treat was a bus ride to downtown Dallas to see a movie at the Majestic,

Palace or Tower theatres. Walking into the Majestic was like entering a world of soft red velvet. The huge organ would pop out of the floor. I can still feel the excitement.

I remember the Webers root beer stand. This is another time when if you happened to be in the small category, you got a small icey frosted root beer. The older ones got the big ones. In due time I grew to this category.

Remember how hot the Dallas summers were especially before air-conditioning? One day, Mom asked me to run around to the 7-Eleven and buy a coke. When I returned with that ice cold coca cola, she called all the children into the kitchen. She sat on her high stool and gave each one of us a sip. Then I watched as she took two very small sips to empty the bottle. She had an ahh moment. It was a really hot day and the ringlets around her neck were moist. Here is where I learned what is means to share.

We prayed the family Rosary quite a lot. I was little, and don't remember my age, but I couldn't stand to say all those Hail Marys. I noticed dad didn't count heads at Rosary time, so I just took myself quickly down the hall and hid under my bed. After several attempts at this scheme, it must have been my guardian angel, because I heard this voice inside me, "don't you know that God is everywhere and he expects you in there with your family?" OK, I said to myself, I'll start next time.

I asked Jesus and His Blessed Mother to pleeeese help me and they did.

Many years later, after not reciting this particular prayer, one day I was driving along and out of the blue, the subject of the Rosary just popped into my head. Oh, my goodness! So being in the present moment, with an open heart, I began to recall this intercessory prayer to the Blessed Mother. After all, it involves the contemplation of her Son, Jesus, my Lord and Savior. After all, she has asked us to pray it. By golly, it's not about do I feel like it or do I want to pray it, but the Mother of our God is asking this of me. Then I started thinking of the mysteries and couldn't remember them all.

128

The next day I was talking to one of my friends. She told me that at Church the previous Sunday, she found a brochure on the floor that had all the mysteries of the Rosary in it. Did I want it? Wow! Of course, then, the next day I was driving and the Hail Mary prayer just popped out of my mouth real slow. Oh Blessed Mother, thank you. After several days of praying my new found Rosary, I began to think, why not remind my family so I did just that.

Then, I began to think about the church members. One day after Mass, I walked up to our Pastor and reminded him that the Blessed Mother wants us to pray the Rosary, and that I did not see any information on this anywhere. Father told me that October is the month of the Holy Rosary; could I wait until then to see about this matter? "No Father, the Blessed Mother would not be pleased if we sit around and wait 4 more months." He referred me to the lady in charge of the Christian Doctrine. I made an appointment with her but thought I could get copies of that brochure. I called the 800 number on the back and it was disconnected. Well, I tried. Several days later, the thought entered my head to just go ahead and have copies made and so I did, 500 on blue paper. I told the sales person it was very important to print this brochure on blue paper. Whatever you say lady!

The appointment day rolled around and Rosemary received me graciously. I asked her if we could put the brochures out in the vestibule of the Church and she agreed. Then, I asked her if she had any rosaries lying around, and sure enough, she had a basket full in her storage room. Can you get them out? First though have Father bless them. I asked Rosemary to replace the brochures when necessary. She promised she would. On my way home, I was filled with great joy and thanked my Holy Spirit for His guidance in the matter. The rosaries and brochures were indeed placed on the table and were gone in a couple of months.

I'm reminded of another time I went into some store. When checking out, the young man behind the counter was staring at my Blessed Mother medal. So I lifted it up and said to him,

"This is Mary, the Mother of Jesus." "Oh, you must be one of those Catholics," he said. Then I said, "You know she's your mother too." I smiled as he was still for a few seconds. Then he proceeded to check me out. On the way home I was in touch with Our Lady with a little prayer for that guy.

Mom had milk delivered from the Metzger Milk Company. Back then, the milk wagon was drawn by a horse. She received a yearly citation from this company for being the customer with the highest order for milk, and for this she received some free milk.

Her ice box was just that, a brown wooden frame box, The ice man came down the side of the house with that black, rubber pad on his back, into the back door, and distributed a huge block of ice into one side of the box. This cooled off the food in the next chamber (By the way, when mom passed away, the ice man called me. He remembered our mother as being so gracious and friendly with that twinkly smile.)

I remember when we got a brand new Bendix washing machine. Prior to this we scrubbed clothes in the bath tub. Then we had that open, round machine with the roller off to the side. You had to be careful not to get your hand caught. Anyway, dad asked mom to save some of her wash for Saturday morning when this new machine would arrive. All of us sat around the kitchen floor and watched the demonstration, given by dad. It was truly a remarkable day. How exciting to see those clothes tumbling and tumbling, through that little window. We still had to hang up all those clothes to dry out back. I thought we would never finish that day.

I want to take a moment and talk about the clothes line. There are some basic rules you know:

1. You had to wash the clothes line before hanging any clothes on it.
2. You had to hang the clothes in a certain order, whites with whites.
3. You never hung a shirt by the shoulders, always by the tail.

4. Hang the sheets and towels on the outside lines so you could hide your unmentionables in the middle.
5. It didn't matter if it was really cold out...clothes would freeze dry.
6. If you were efficient, you would line the clothes up so that each item did not need 2 clothes pins, but shared one of the pins with next item.
7. Clothes off the line before dinner, neatly folded and ready to be ironed.
8. Ironed??????? Well, that's a whole other subject.

A POEM

A clothesline was a news forecast
To neighbors passing by,
There were no secrets you could keep
When clothes were hung to dry.
It also was a friendly link
For neighbors always knew
If company had stopped on by
To spend a night or two.
For then you'd see the fancy sheets
And towels upon the line;
You'd see the company tablecloths
With intricate design.
The line announced a baby's birth
To folks who lived inside
As brand new infant clothes were hung
So carefully with pride.
The ages of the children could
So readily be known
By watching how the sizes changed
You'd know how much they'd grown.
It also told when illness struck,
As extra sheets were hung;
Then nightclothes, and a bathrobe, too,
Haphazardly were strung.

It said, gone on vacation now
When lines were limp and bare.
It told,' we're back!' when full lines sagged
With not an inch to spare.
I really miss that way of life.
It was a friendly sign
When neighbors knew each other best
By what hung on the line.

(Author Unknown)

Several years later dad purchased our first air-conditioner. It was placed in the living room. That night, we all slept in the living room, not a space left to walk thru. What a relief from the hot Dallas summers. I remember taking turns sleeping by the window with my sister, Joanne. We would place a wet towel on our back so that the slightest breeze would cool us off.

Now, I'm just going to continue. Remember bobby pins, penny loafers, bobby socks, saddle oxfords, pony tails, sweater sets, cinch belts, ship-n-shore blouses, neck scarves, crinoline slips, full skirts, cotton shirt dresses, grey and red outfit, hats, gloves, nylons with the seam up the back, black, patent leather "Mary Jane" shoes, Buster Brown shoe stores with the x-ray machines , to see where the toes were ?

The radio was a part of our life. The Hit Parade, The Shadow Knows, Fibber McGee and Molly, The Lone Ranger, Burns and Allen, Sherlock Holmes, Life of Riley, Jack Benny, Hop-along Cassidy, The Baby Snook's Show, Fred Allen, My Friend Irma, Our Miss Brooks, The Green Hornet, Duffy's Tavern, Radio City Playhouse, Announcer Howard Duff, Ford Theater, Amos and Andy, Mystery In The Air, hosted by Peter Lorre, American Novels on ABC, Adventures of Sam Spade with Howard Duff playing the title spot, Dragnet with Jack Webb, The Hallmark Playhouse, Lux Radio Theater, and Night Beat with Frank Lovejoy.

When some of our friends would drop by for a visit, it wasn't long when if you peaked over the top of the french doors which were opened slightly at the top, you would see four or five pairs of little eyes taking in the scene.

I mentioned the 12 foot-long dinner table. Dad got it from St. Mary's University. We sat on two sets of 6 foot benches on either side. Mom was at one end, dad at the other. The little kids were interspersed between older ones. Mom always prepared several bowls of vegetables and by the time the bowl got to the other end of the table, it could be empty. The same held true if you started the bowl at your end of the table, you probably got a nice size serving, but the ones at the other end may have lost out.

Our Mother made what we called oven fried chicken. She started frying the chicken as usual and placed the pieces in the oven to keep warm as she fried up more. By the time we ate them, they were so tender and juicy. The little ones picked their pieces first which were always the thighs and drumsticks. It could happen that only 3 or 4 wings were left for one of us older kids.

It seems we always had enough to eat though. Saturday, at noon, was hamburger time. Fridays, since we did not eat meat, mom prepared a long 13 by 9 inch pan of macaroni, swimming in Hunt's tomato sauce, with melted cheddar cheese on top. Sometimes we had tomato soup with grilled cheese sandwiches. She fixed the best Hungarian goulash, with red kidney beans, tomato soup hamburger meat and macaroni. I loved the boiled eggs on top of the spinach. Sunday was roast beef day. At least once a week dad would fix his famous spaghetti and meatballs. Another favorite was mom's fresh green beans, new potatoes with ham hocks. She made the ham, potato and cheddar cheese dish swimming in milk. This she learned from Grandmother O'Brien. She would use that 13 by 9 inch pan and bake a yellow cake with real fudge icing. I still have her large yellow Pyrex bowl that she filled with potato salad. She would cut up bananas in jello. Other times she made yummy apple salad.

Once again, I thank God for these memories that will pass from generation to generation.

THE NEIGHBORHOOD
4427 BOWSER AVE.
DALLAS, TEXAS, 75219

We moved from Garrett Avenue in Dallas, to Bowser Avenue, when I was around three years of age. In fact, my sister, Eileen, was born the day after we moved in, June 1, 1941. The white frame house was to become the home for all of us McCaffrey kids, 14 in all living at the time. The two older boys, Jim and Pat, lived in the servant quarters out back.

Across the front of the house was a wide open porch. The concrete was nice and smooth for roller skating. It seems we were always losing the metal key to tighten the skates to our shoes until someone thought to string an old shoe lace through the top of the key. Oh, the hours we spent on those skates. We had to share you know, but that was par for the course. The concrete was great for the crispy bounce of the golf ball when we played jacks. I loved the ping sound of the ball and those metal jacks as they fell every which way.

During the summer months, the shaded area on the porch was just right for our mother who took her place there in the afternoons after our nap.

Mom had a regular routine. In the morning we played in the back yard. After lunch, we all took our naps, while mom rested too. She had such good common sense. As we grew out of sleeping for a nap, we still had to rest. We would play word and color games in bed. Then we got our bath and put on fresh clothes. As I got older, I helped mom line up those white, high top shoes, and polish them. She would boil up the starch for the shirts, and then they got ironed.

The next morning we played again in the back yard. The clothes from the day before got washed and the clean ones laid out all in a row. The blue eyed kids wore pastels, and the brown eyed kids wore beige and yellow. It was exciting when dad arrived home each day. We were all out in front to greet him. One day dad saw me chasing a squirrel around a big tree out by the curb. From then on, I was named "Squirrely". He loved attaching nick names to us.

The driveway was to the left of the house and ended up way in the back, right into the garage. Along the side of the driveway was a long, white picket fence covered with climbing red roses. I never knew if these flowers were ours or the neighbors. Anyway, mom nursed them along each season, pruning them back in the fall. She always nourished her plants and flowers with careful pruning and watering between rains, just like she nourished and cared for her children.

The sweet smell of honeysuckle along the back fence pleased our senses. Two pecan trees shaded the back side of the house. We loved those nuts. Mom used them when she made her fudge, which was another of her routines. It was exciting to watch the chocolate boil up and we took turns checking the little ball in the cold water, to see if it was time to start beating. She would pour the chocolate out into a buttered pie dish. If you were one of the little ones, you got to clean the pot with a spoon. Since I was one of the older ones, eventually I had to step aside and watch my little brothers and sisters go at it. There was a great joy in watching and sharing with the little ones.

Getting back to the pecan trees. We used the long stems as our hula skirts for our Hawaian dances and we would put on shows for the neighbors.

We had a small swing set out back and a sand box. In the fall, we would pile up the leaves and swing out and jump into the leaves. I loved the crackling sound.

Across the street from our house was a two story, red- brick house. Soon a family moved in downstairs. The grandfather was placed out in front. Goodness knows he had a lot to observe with all us kids coming and going. One day I went over to say hello. Then I made it a point to drop by more often. We seemed to enjoy each other's company. I was around 9 or 10. One day, the sky was extra blue, and the clouds all puffed up, and I remember telling him how great God the Father is for creating such a wonderful world for us. I asked if he believed in God and he did. So, we got to talk about God a lot. Then, one day, he asked to speak to my dad. Sometime after that, dad took him to church several times, and he was baptized. He died soon after that. Oh, I thought, someday I will meet him again.

We had really nice neighbors. Mary Ann Triece lived next door and she later married my cousin Don Vogel.

The Brunson family lived on the corner. My sister JoAnne and I played with Marie, Jeaneen, and Bettye Sue. We played dress-up in their back yard, and played jacks, and skated together. At one time, we started collecting the jokers of various card decks. Mrs. Brunson had a garden beside her house and grew some vegetables for canning. One of them was okra, and I never quite liked the slimy taste. Its ok if fried.

During the summer we would all pile on a blanket or two and my dad would tell us the most outlandish ghost stories.

I want to tell this story about my brother Skip. One summer evening, he went to bed early because he was tired. You see, he had a plan. Dad caught on real quick. Thinking that everyone had turned in for the night, Skip slipped out the window, leaving a match stick in the corner of the screen so he could get back in. He returned later on, slipped back through the window, and tip toed to his bed. When he pulled back the covers, there was dad lying there to greet him. Ah ha, he was caught red handed.

The Vicks lived around the corner from us. Mr. Vick was the butcher at the Safeway store, where my mom shopped. Mrs. Vick repaired woolen clothes and could darn the fabric like new. Their daughter, Diane, was an excellent gymnast.

There was a 7-Eleven store around the corner on Lemon Avenue. It is still there to this day. We would collect coke bottles and sell them there to get a treat or two.

Whatever treat was purchased, was shared equally among all.

There was a three story white hotel across from the 7-Eleven. Periodically, on a weekend, my dad would check himself in with his books, for a little rest. I was his little secretary. I would walk over, go in the back door, knock on his door and deliver his messages. Then he gave me a hug and off I went. Later on, I thought what a common sense thing to do.

Mom shopped several blocks away off Lemon Avenue. The Skillern drug store had that fantastic soda fountain, with the red, black and white decor; the shiny silver fountains and the roundabout stools. What fun to share malts with a friend or two.

Next door was Ashburn's Ice Cream Store. I loved their lemon custard. Later, the store moved to Highland Park.

There was a women's dress shop at the end of that strip mall. They accepted lay-a-way. In my junior year in high school, for the Jesuit Homecoming Dance, I went there with my two sisters, Eileen and Angela, to get me a new outfit. I was to pay down and put the rest in lay-a-way. So, it happened that I noticed my sisters looking at matching peacock blue and brown corduroy skirts and tops. Never mind me, I thought, and decided that we should buy those outfits for them. They were thrilled. Anyway, I had already been to two previous homecoming dances. This was their first high school big deal dance.

This reminds me, on another evening, driving in the neighborhood, it was during the winter and very cold. My mom had bought her four teen-age daughters, JoAnne, Angela, Eileen and myself, two short coats, one baby blue for Angela and I, and one beige for JoAnne and Eileen. I was wearing the blue coat on a certain evening out. I noticed this girl on the street corner selling flowers, and she had only a sweater on. "Oh no", I said, "stop the car." I got out and gave her my coat. The next day, I simply told mom that now we only had one coat for the four of us. I told her not to worry, we would manage. After all we had sweaters.

I couldn't talk about our neighborhood without mentioning Stephen J. Hay School and park, about three blocks up

137

Hawthorne from our house. Some family had a pear tree jutting out across the side walk, so it was real easy to take a sample as we passed by.

I spent hours and hours at this park during grade school. There was an organized and supervised swim program. I learned to swim early and won quite a few ribbons during the annual city wide swim meet. I would whip up a raw egg in milk with a teaspoon of sugar before the meets. This sustained my energy level. For years my sister, Margaret Ann, wondered about this "raweggnmilk" drink. Later on, I swam for Highland Park and the Dallas Athletic Club. During the summer I would get up early and walk way over to the Highland Park pool to train. To strengthen our respiratory system we would swim as far as possible under water. The farthest I got was a length and a half of the pool. Mom was never able to get to the meets but she sure was happy with me upon my victorious return home. Dad came several times to watch.

The park had a crackerjack softball team. I played shortstop and was always fourth batter in the batting lineup, so I could usher home the loaded bases. We played teams all over Dallas and usually won.

I loved croquet and paddle ball. The arts and crafts programs were good but I never quite got into those activities. I was always playing some kind of sport.

The summer after the 5th grade, I met a special friend at the park. His name was Joel. He wore a little black cap on his head so I knew he was Jewish. I thought he was real cute. He had black curly hair with freckles across his nose. Once I told him that we have something in common. I remember he just looked at me. I guess he was wondering what? What? – We both have freckles, his across his nose and mine all over my face. I told him that my dad called my freckles "angel kisses".

At that time, my dad was active in the National Conference of Christians and Jews. Joel and I would sit on the curb and have all kinds of discussions. Once, I was telling him that for the life of me, I could not understand that his people did not accept Jesus as their Messiah. After all, he was Jewish too. Now, all these years they have been waiting around. He didn't say much about that. Dad came home from work that day as usual. I introduced Joel to him. Dad invited him to stay for supper, but he couldn't. I told my dad about our discussions, and he told me to remember our Jewish friends in my prayers, that God loved them dearly. So, all these years they have remained in my prayers. I wonder what Joel is doing today.

Aunt Una lived down the street. She was quite a character from New York and used to be in Vaudeville. She had a high voice, always had this tight, curly perm, bright red lipstick, and in the summer wore sundresses and socks with sandals. Every afternoon she would walk down the street with her empty six-pack of cokes, heading for the 7-Eleven around the corner. I would wonder how such a tiny woman could imbibe so many cokes in one day. Since we were always out in front with mom, she always stopped by to visit. I'm sure mom enjoyed her visits. At Christmas time we were invited into her living room to view (but not touch) anything. There was a tiny toy train around a village surrounding the Christmas tree. It was so beautiful. This was one of those traditional happenings. I remember there were delicate glass figurines all over the place, and we wouldn't dare disturb any of them. I never saw any dust either. Aunt Una kept up with us even after we moved out of the neighborhood to 10520 Gooding Drive, in North Dallas. As my sisters married, she would send them baby gifts. We all loved Aunt Una.

Sports came easy to me. Early on, at the age of 4 and 5, Aunt Una's daughter, little Una, took me under her wing and provided ice skating lessons for me. Una bought my skates and even had two velvet outfits made for me, one was a black velvet skirt lined in red taffeta, with a white blouse; the other was a blue-green velvet full short dress, with white fuzzy fur around the hem, neck and sleeves. I have pictures so that's how come I can remember this. Una would curl my usually straight hair with a hot curling iron, or roll it in pieces of white cloth and presto, Shirley Temple curls.

URSULA THE SKATER

To this day I can vividly remember the rising excitement as we neared the ice arena. I always carried my skates over my shoulder. You could hear the music as the lace up ritual took place. Then the bouncy steps came next as I made my way thru those doors out into the rink. A rush of cool air hit my face and off I went!

I had to suffer through the skating lesson in the beginning, doing those boring figure eights. I did learn that old adage, "practice makes perfect". Then came the free- skate session. What a thrill to take off and sail around the rink in rhythm to the music.

We had partner sessions too, and we swayed back and forth in long glides. The airplane was always so graceful, with the left leg held high out the back. I managed mini jumps, the bottom squat, and slow twirls. I never did get the fast spins.

Across the street from the 7-Eleven, and half way down the block was the dental office of Dr.Philip Rodriquez. He went to St. Mary's University with dad. He was always so gracious. Every now and then dad would announce that several of us were scheduled to walk over to get our teeth checked. I had soft, bad teeth like mom. So, on more than one occasion, I would keep walking slowly by the office and head for home. I knew the good doctor didn't know exactly which one of us was due to show up. I had a hard time with that shot and the drill!

It seems that we had a roller rink somewhere nearby. The excitement grew as we stepped inside the dimly lit rink, with those rotating balls of light. The organ music was blaring forth, and I couldn't wait to get my skates laced up and off I went gliding around with my hair and skirt blowing in the breeze.

This leads me to mention at this time, our family meetings that took place at 4427 Bowser Avenue. About once a month, we all gathered in the living room. Mom sat in that certain chair off to the side. I watched her all the time. She sat so graciously with her hands folded gently. Dad would begin our meeting with a prayer, and a Christian teaching, to love one another, to look out for our neighbor. (Here is where I got the idea to visit that old man across the street.) Then he would change our chores around. Once, as he assigned a duty to one of us, he glanced at mom and she said, "Jim McCaffrey, you better not put me on any list." Dad smiled and proceeded to the next assignment.

I used to watch exchanges between my parents. It was interesting, and if any of us were not up to snuff regarding our chores, we were quietly reminded.

TEXAS

*S*ince I was born and raised in Dallas, Texas, I thought I would give it a little praise and be true to my roots. You say you're from Texas and folks ask about cowboys, cattle, horses and the like. Yep, we got them too. It's plenty big and spread out so the land takes shape in all kinds of ways – the piney woods, mountains in the Big Bend, bluebonnets nodding back and forth in the Hill Country, warm beaches down on the Gulf Coast, the Ft. Worth stock yards, huge herds of cattle roaming the ranges, Mexican food that'll knock yer socks off, the Alamo, where 185 brave men standing in a church facing 1500 Mexican nationals, fighting for freedom, who had a chance to walk out and save themselves but remained till the last man fell. The famous "Remember the Alamo" battle cry remains forever etched in history. While this battle was going on it bought time for Sam Houston to prepare his troops for a victory against Santa Ana's army at San Jacinto.

Texas is Juneteenth and Texas Independence Day. There are many schools named after Sam Houston, William B. Travis, Davy Crockett, the king of the wild frontier.

We got those shiny skyscrapers in Dallas and Houston. Can't forget the flat plains out West around Midland and Lubbock dotted with oil wells some of which are sittin there nice and quiet.

Some towns and cities shut down for the Friday night high school football games. I'm remembering the Jesuit pep rallies out front of the old school on Oak Lawn Ave. I loved the excitement, the cheers, and the band and of course the players always added a certain interest.

Now here's a little bit of trivia. By federal law, Texas is the only State in the U.S. that flies its flag at 20 feet. Do you know why? Well, because it is the only State that was a Republic before it became a State.

The Johnson Space Center in Houston has heralded many explorations into space.

Yes siree the stars at night are big and bright, deep in the heart of Texas. The sage in bloom is like perfume, deep in the heart of Texas.

I mentioned before that when Mom and Dad returned to Texas with their two little sons, Jim and Pat, Dad got down on his knees and kissed the earth after they crossed the border into Texas. Remember he was born in Waco and Mom in Dallas. They were home! I want to say thank you again to Our Heavenly Father for so many blessings to our family as we all were brought forth to live and move and have our beings united with Him and His Son and our Holy Spirit.

MY EARLY YEARS

*T*he day of my birth took place October 20, 1938 at 10:53 AM at the old St Paul Hospital on Hall St. in Dallas, Texas. I was delivered by Uncle Dennis MD (brother of my Grandmother Wilson), the 5th living child weighing in at a hearty 8 lbs. Thank you Heavenly Father for the start of this most precious life. Jim, Pat, Mary Elise (who died at 18 months), Joanne and Skippy preceded me. Charles Joseph was born November 25, 1936 and lived long enough for Uncle Dennis to baptize him.

Mom was 28 and dad was 29. They rented an apartment at 1421 Bennett Ave from my Grandfather Wilson. Dad was a salesman for Pittsburgh Plate Glass Co; mom was home with her children.

November 13, 1938 I received the Sacrament of Baptism at Sacred Heart Cathedral. This day becomes a cause of celebration within my very soul. Rev. father J.M. Wiewell performed the service. The practice of infant Baptism is an immemorial tradition in my Church. There is an explicit testimony to this practice from the second century on and it is possible that, from the beginning of the apostolic preaching, when whole households received Baptism, infants were apparently included. (Acts 16:15, 33, 18:8)

All Eastern and most Western churches consider infant baptism as having been the norm from the beginning of the Christian era. The great theologian Origen, for example, about the year 280 AD and St Augustine, about 400 AD, considered infant baptism a "tradition" received from the apostles.

We had more and more children join our family: Angela,

Eileen, Mike, Don, Steve, Margaret Ann, Christine, Tom and Philip. My sister Dorothy Genevieve was a full term stillborn on November 30, 1950. There never was a dull moment. What fun it was to share life with all these characters. Then there was dad with his sense of humor and mom with her gracious quiet ways topped it all off.

ANGELA – EILEEN – URSULA AT TOP

Dad would line us all up and promised a nickel or dime to the child who would not laugh while he counted our ribs. Do you know Skip won every time? He would move his mouth over to the side like Spanky and not a peep came out of him. Myself, I started giggling just walking up to the plate so to speak. Dad made the most outlandish funny faces even before he started counting.

I was 5 when the first Lassie movie came out, "Lassie Come Home". Lassie is a girl but the role was always played by a male dog, the first named Pal. All the Lassie descendents were from Pal's line. The male dog was used because of the shiny coat.

Christmas was the greatest! We all lined up outside the living room with blind folds on holding on to the shoulder of the one in front of you. Dad would go ahead of us into the room making tin-kly noises and shaking some of the boxes with his oohs and ahs. It seemed like the longest time passed until the march started into the room. Oh my goodness! It was sooo exciting. Next came the countdown and the blind folds just flew all over the room. A most magnificent scene lay before us. We shared a lot of our gifts like the pair of roller skates, the doll, a bike and games. There was the manger scene at the bottom of the tree. I used to think wow what a way to celebrate the birth of Jesus. Later on as I got older, I began to understand more of what this means.

All of heaven rejoices on this day. Thank you Heavenly Father for sending us Your Son, our Redeemer. Christ's whole earthly life reveals you. Jesus said, "Whoever has seen me sees the Father."

Since there were nine more brothers and sisters who followed me, it was even more joyful to play "Santa Claus". We always set out the milk and cookies. Mom read "Twas the Night before Christmas". Later on I discovered that the toys were in that big hall closet at Grandpa's house.

The Jesuit scholastics built us a train set with a little village surrounding the track. They used household items, for example a small coffee can painted green with a black rubber tube hanging out, was the water tower. I never dreamed we would have our own train set. We had been admiring Aunt Una's train set for years.

We all went to Sunday Mass together. I remember receiving a new dress for Christmas and Easter, gifts from our Grandmother Wilson. These dresses were saved for Sunday worship time. Some of them were handed on to the next in line.

Every year the season of Lent managed to roll around. We thought we really sacrificed, giving up candy, doughnuts, desserts and movies. We went to daily Mass sometimes with our parents, other times at school. On Good Friday from 12 pm to 3 pm Mom kept everybody at home as quiet as possible in honor of Jesus hanging on the cross for us. When I got old enough to attend the reading of the Passion at Church, I stood very still. I loved the veneration of the crucifix and would think, my, how Jesus loves me.

It is one of the traditions in our Church that we wear sacramentals, medals and crucifixes. Sacramentals are special prayers, actions or objects, the use of which obtains spiritual benefits through the prayers of the Church to God. People wear various pins to signify their affiliation with some club or allegiance to the country using an American flag pin. So we show our allegiance to our church using various religious symbols.

After Lent we celebrated the feast of the Risen Lord. Easter Sunday was so special. Christ rose from the dead to show that He is truly God and to teach us that we, too, shall rise from the dead. He did not rise by the power of His human nature, but by the power of His divine nature, which He shares with the Father and the Holy Spirit.

Traditionally we received our Easter baskets. They were hidden all over the place. Then we got to don our new outfits. Another special joy was shared by all as our dad, who left on Wednesday of Holy Week for his annual retreat at the Monastery in Conyers, Ga., returned home for Easter. Yes, we were happy that Jesus finally completed His mission here on this earth and we could rejoice that our dad was refreshed in body, mind and spirit. I could see the light in his eyes as I got older.

It is August 21, 2008 and I discovered just today some spiritual notes our dad wrote while at his retreat in Georgia. I was glancing at several albums when my eye fixed on a certain one. When I opened it I thought what is this? There were pictures of relatives. I almost put it back when I felt urged to keep turning those pages. His notes were in the back of the album. I will now let everyone know what dad wrote in his own hand about our life in Grace:

WITH THE GRACE OF GOD
1) Try and keep Christ in everything I do.
2) Leave all negative aspects of daily living up to Christ.
3) Daily Mass
4) Morning Offering
5) Keep calm in the confidence that Christ is in on everything ; I am on the right.
6) Make everything do – actually a prayer.
7) Thank God for the opportunities, gifts as often as I ask Him for favors.

Grace: Is the one important thing one _must_ have to save his soul.

Christ said to St. Peter – I have forgiven you. I have forgotten your sins. You have work to do.

Knowledge of the ways of perfection and most importantly strength of Will – to follow out the plan of perfection.

Prudence: Means to me in my circumstances – to use means available to me in my station in life to sanctify my soul.

Therefore, work hard without waste of time or worry, to love, mainly to be used strictly as a means of perfection.

Do the job within the bounds of loving, knowing and serving God – also this is the only way for happiness or attaining heaven.

God has a whole plan for your life. Meditation makes it possible for you to conform your activities to His plan.

149

SINGING

I want to mention in more detail how much I loved to sing and I'll be naming some of my favorite songs. When we had our little back yard performances for the neighbors, I always sang 2 or 3 songs and pantomimed the words. Here goes!

Oh would you like to swing on a star, carry moonbeams home in a jar,
And be better off then you are or would you rather be a mule.
A mule is an animal that kicks up his heels and I don't remember the rest.

"Look For the Silver Lining"….. "Skip To My Lou"….. "My Bonnie Lies Over The Ocean" ….. "I'm Back In The Saddle Again" – Gene Autry …..
"Shine On Harvest Moon" ….. "Skip To My Lou" ….. "Don't Sit Under The Apple Tree" ….. "We Were Sailing Along" ….. "Look For The Silver Lining" ….. "Lollipop" – The Chordettes ….. "26 Miles Across The Sea" – The 4 Preps ….. "Little Darlin" – The Diamonds ….. "Goodnight Sweetheart" – The McGuire Sisters ….. "At The End Of The Rainbow" – Johnny Mathis ….. "Music Music Music" – Theresa Brewer ….. "Que Sera Sera" – Doris Day ….. "Mr Sandman" – The Chordettes ….. "Catch A Falling Star" – Perry Como ….. "Glow Worm" – Mills Brothers ….. "Mambo Italiano" & "Hey There" – Rosemary Clooney ….. "Tennessee Waltz" – Pattie Page ….. "Buttons and Bows" – Dinah Shore ….. "Shaboom" ….. "Wheel Of Fortune" – Kay Starr ….. "Peg O My Heart"

150

….. "Daisy Daisy" ….. "Three Coins In The Fountain" – 4 Aces ….."Remember When" – The Platters

These are just a few and I really enjoyed singing and dancing to the melodies.

GRADE SCHOOL

*W*e lived about 8 or 9 blocks from Holy Trinity Grade School, run by the Daughters of Charity of St Vincent DePaul and the Vincentian Fathers. The school was founded in 1914 to serve the needs of the working class families who were anxious to hand on their Catholic faith to the next generation. Fr. Stanton was our Pastor. He showed up on the play ground all the time, hiked up his cassock, and we would chase him laughing all the while.

The sisters wore the "holy habit" as they described it. We marveled at the big white starched coronet that covered the head with a big white collar and bib. The dress was navy blue. There was the biggest rosary ever hanging from the side belt. How I loved these sisters. I really lucked out every year as I liked all my teachers. My favorite was Sister Mary Angela. She was peppy, joyful, and truly interested in us all. When she spoke to me, it was like no one else was around.

We wore a school uniform, white blouse with blue tie ribbon, navy blue skirt and sweater, blue and white saddle oxfords with bobby socks. This really helped the family budget especially since we could pass on the uniform to the next in line.

I remember Sister Gertrude was my first grade teacher. She was short in stature. We learned to read from the Dick and Jane series. The highlight of that year was my First Holy Communion day when I got to receive Jesus under the appearance of that little white consecrated bread. In the Bible Jesus said, "This **IS** My Body". He didn't say this looks like My Body. "It is by the conversion of the bread and wine into Christ's body and blood that Christ becomes present in this sacrament. The early Church Fathers strongly affirmed the faith of the Church in the efficacy of the Word of Christ and the action of the Holy Spirit to bring about this conversion." (Taken from Catechism of the Catholic Church paragraph 1375.)

FIRST HOLY COMMUNION DAY

The "Holy Eucharist" is the Body, Blood Soul and Divinity of Jesus Christ. It is the source and summit of our faith.

I prepared all year for this day. My mother would instruct me step by step. I had been listening to my older brothers and sister prepare for their First Communions. Oh, I thought soon it would be my turn. I wore a lovely white dress and veil as was the custom to signify the purity of the heart.

It just so happened that our dad had a Knights of Columbus baseball game scheduled at the lower Jesuit campus on that day. We didn't have time for me to go home and change so off we went to the game. It didn't take long before I began climbing up the rocks and true to form, I managed to tear my dress picking up some of the red dust too. There I was again in the present moment with focus on getting up to the top of the rocks. This was par for the course. My mom never got angry. This wasn't the first time I came home disheveled.

The grade school lunches were always good. Dad purchased lunch cards for us. He must have been given some kind of discount or something because thru the years he always had a bunch of kids in the school.

My physical education classes were a fun part of the day. Agility was one of my strong points as I advanced in the tumbling class. We played baseball before classes even started. There was a mini soccer field alongside the telephone building and us girls played what we called speedball. I could kick that ball soaring over the heads of the players and right thru the goal post!

Dad would call the school to make an appointment with the Principal so he could get reports on us all. He did not have time to go one by one to all those parent/teacher conferences. He was accommodated and I looked forward to getting my report. Once he told me the teacher said I had an ability for quiet leadership. That suited me just fine as I wasn't about to step up and be heard. I was a bit shy about public speaking.

Around 7 or 8 I helped my mother with the little ones. I remember she came home from the hospital in an ambulance after a 5 or 6 day stay for childbirth. How exciting as we waited outside and watched that long ambulance, with the small glass windows on either side, move slowly up the street to our house. Mom would be transferred from the ambulance directly to her bed with our little brother or sister tucked snugly to her side. She remained on bed rest for several more days. No wonder she was a bit weak when she finally got up. I was taught how to boil the baby bottles and mix up the formula using powder, water and karo syrup. No one was allowed in her room for one week except me to bring in the formula.

Here's a little trivia. In 1947, Jackie Robinson was the first Afro-American to play in major league baseball. I was nine years old and counting.

This reminds me that Dad provided Mom with some help when we were small. Ruby Lee and then later on Lucille were the ladies that pitched in to help. They always came in the back door. I didn't understand that until later on boy was I happy that Rosa Parks got on that bus and sat where she wanted to way up in front. Little did I know at the time that I would have the awesome privilege of serving the black man in his native habitat.

I remember singing all the day long. I loved to sing! Every year at school we celebrated St. Patrick's Day in a big way. We Irish kids jumped right into the middle of it all. Pat Shine and I sang an Irish ditty once. You have to admit that those songs just placed a little joy into the heart and a big smile on the face.

By golly, I think that now I would like to share some Irish Blessings:

May you always have work for your hands to do,
May your pockets hold always a coin or two,
May the sun shine bright on your window pane,
May the rainbow be certain to follow each rain,
May the hand of a friend always be near you,
And may God fill your heart with gladness to cheer you.

May the raindrops fall lightly on your brow:
May the soft winds freshen your spirit;
May the sunshine brighten your heart;
May the burdens of the day rest lightly upon you;
May God enfold you in the mantle of His love.

May you always find blue skies above your head,
Shamrocks beneath your feet, laughter and joy aplenty,
Kindness from all you meet, good friends and kin to miss you
If ever you choose to roam, and a path that's been cleared
By the angels themselves to carry you safely home.

155

Wishing you always walls for the wind,
And a roof for the rain, and tea beside the fire,
Laughter to cheer you, and those you love near you,
And all that your heart might desire.

Deep peace of the running waves to you.
Deep peace of the flowing air to you.
Deep peace of the smiling stars to you.
Deep peace of the quiet earth to you.
Deep peace of the watching shepherds to you.
Deep peace of the Son of Peace to you.

May you never find trouble
All crowdin and shovin'But always good fortune –
All smiling and lovin'.
I could go on and on but you all get the drift.

Through the years I joined whatever choirs were available. I can still see Mrs. Clark up in the choir loft accompanying us on the organ. We had music lessons at school but I never could read the notes on the scale; I sang by ear. Just let me hear the melody once and I will know it. Harmonizing was no problem.

Some of us in the neighborhood would prepare a program in the back yard and charge a nickel entrance fee. We would sing and pantomime various songs. All talents were welcome. We placed a blanket over the clothesline for the curtain.

We played hop scotch a lot and jumped rope till the sun set. We sat facing each other for the hand clapping game singing this ditty: My name is Arabella, I come from the land of jella, with a pickle on my nose and a cherry on my toes, my name is Arabell la la la. With the little ones we would clap their hands and sing Patty cake patty cake bakers man, bake me a cake as fast as you can. Roll em up and roll em up and throw em in the pan. This brought a lot of laughter and of course the little ones would say "do it again"!

After supper we played hide-n-seek. Can't forget the roller skates. Dodge ball was a favorite as we got older. Then there was tag, Simon says and blind man's bluff. We would spend a couple of hours trying to pick up one of those sticks without touching the rest. I didn't keep track of time much especially during the long hot summer months unless my tummy signaled it's time to eat. Remember I was always in the present moment.

Oh, the Drive-In-Theater! What fun! The first one debuted in Camden N.J.; they peaked in the 50's with 5,000. That big sound box that hung on the car door was adequate.

On Saturdays we had to have our housework done by noon so we could go to the Esquire Theater to see Roy Rogers or Gene Autry. I can remember the bolo contests; you know when you bat the little red ball attached to a long rubber, up and down with a paddle. This was a fad for awhile.

Talking about fads, what about the yo yo. There were varying degrees of expertise on those things. I used to marvel at the "rock the baby" routine or "walk the dog". It was all in the flip of the wrist.

Once Mom & Dad took us out to White Rock Lake to swim. We had the best time ever. So everybody climbed into that wood paneled station wagon to return home except me. I was way out in the lake swimming my heart out. After arriving home, I was discovered missing. Dad dashed back to find me having the time of my life. Yep I was in the present moment all right.

Father McGrath S.J. presented our family with a really huge picture of the Sacred Heart of Jesus. Our home was blessed. Dad would give talks to other families about the enthronement of the Sacred heart. This picture took center stage above our mantle in the living room. No matter where you sat or knelt as when we prayed the rosary, the eyes of Jesus were on you; here's lookin at you kid! I even tried to park myself way over in the corner of the room and sure enough, He was right on looking into my very soul.

It just so happened that on a certain day I went up to the Woolworth 5&dime store and slipped a pair of blue socks and a blue ribbon into my pocket. I was in the first or second grade. That evening at Rosary time there was Jesus staring a hole right thru me. I reached into my pocket to feel the stolen goods. After prayers, I just couldn't stand it any longer and asked to speak to my father. He listened to my tale of woe and very calmly took the goods explaining that the next day I would return them to the store manager and express my regret. Dad accompanied me to the store. We walked together up the street a few blocks. He held my hand and we talked about different things not about the socks. The manager accepted my apology and nary a word more was mentioned. How kind and forgiving was my father just like the Heavenly Father.

Every year in the month of May we celebrated the May Procession in honor of the Blessed Mother Mary. Songs were sung in her honor and her statue was crowned with a fresh wreath of flowers. This beautiful tradition has for generations been embraced by the faithful as a special way to honor the Mother of God.

The following is a song for Mary we sang year after year:

ON THIS DAY, O BEAUTIFUL MOTHER

On this day O beautiful Mother, on this day we give thee our love,

Near thee Madonna fondly we hover, trusting thy gentle care to prove.

On this day we ask to share Dearest Mother thy sweet care

Aid us ere our feet astray wander from thy guiding way.

Queen of the angels deign to hear thy dear children's humble prayer,

Young hearts gain O Virgin pure Jesus love for them assures.

Here is the song we always sang for the crowning of Mary:

BRING FLOWERS OF THE RAREST

Bring flow'rs of the fairest; bring flow'rs of the rarest,
From garden and woodland and hillside and vale;
Our full hearts are swelling, our glad voices telling
The praise of the loveliest Rose of the dale.

Chorus:
O Mary! We crown thee with blossoms today
Queen of the Angels, Queen of the May;
O Mary we crown thee with blossoms today,
Queen of the Angels Queen of the May.

This month of May, which like Mary, brings to us new life, abundant fruit and warmth, is widely recognized as her month. This is how we Catholics make visible to the world our devotion to the Mother of God. We do not "worship" her only we reverence her. You see we belong to this Mystical Body of Christ, the Church. We are like a big family and we here on earth are called the Church Militant. We are making our way on this journey toward Heaven. The Church Triumphant is up there already for all eternity in the glory of the Blessed Trinity and in communion with our brothers and sisters in Christ.

You probably have noticed that we Catholics have a lot of images and pictures of the saints, the Blessed Mother, Jesus, His Father and the Holy Spirit. Just like we have pictures of our earthly family, why not our heavenly family? It is true we use all our senses in worshiping our God, the art pieces, the beautiful music, incense and most important our taste as we consume the Body, Blood, Soul and Divinity of Jesus in His Holy Eucharist under the appearance of bread and wine.

As I got older in grade school, the Christmas Novena (nine days from Dec. 17th to the 24th) celebration in Church was so special with the chanting of the "O Antiphons" in Latin prior to the reading of the Gospel:

Dec 17th – **O Wisdom** of our God Most High, guiding creation with power
And love: teach us to walk in the paths of knowledge. (Sapientia
Altissimi, fortiter suaviterque disponens omnia: veni ad
Docendum nos viam prudentiae.)

Dec 18th – **O Leader of the House of Israel**, giver of the Law to Moses
On Sinai: come to rescue us with your mighty power! (Dux
Domus Israel, qui Moysi in Sina legem dedisti: veni ad
Redimentum nos in bracchio extent.)

Dec 19th – **O Root of Jesse's stem**, sign of God's love for all His people:
Come to save us without delay! (Radix Iesse, stans in signum
Populorum: veni ad liberandum nos, iam noli tardare.)

Dec 20th – **O Key of David**, opening the gates of God's eternal Kingdom:
Come and free the prisoners of darkness! (Clavis David, qui
Aperis portas aeterni Regni: veni et educ vinctum de domo
Carceris sedentem in tenebris.)

Dec 21st – **O Emmanuel,** our King and Giver of Law: come to save us, Lord
Our God! (Emmanuel, rex et legifer noster: veni ad salvandum
Nos, Domine, Deus noster.)

Dec 22nd – **O King of all nations** and keystone of the Church: come and
Save man whom you formed from the dust! (Rex gentium et

Lapis angularis Ecclesiae: veni et salva hominem quem de limo
Formasti.)

Dec 23rd – **O let the clouds** rain down the Just One...
(Rorate caeli desuper
Et nubs pluant justum)

Dec 24th – **O Radiant Dawn,** splendor of eternal light, sun of justice: come
And shine on those who dwell in darkness and in the shadow of
Death. (Oriens, splendor lucis aeternae et sol justitiae: veni at
Illumine sedentes in tenebris et umbra mortis.)

The Entrance Antiphons at the beginning of the Holy Mass for these nine days were very special as we anticipated the coming of the Messiah! :

Dec 17th – Laetentur caeli et exulted terra, quia Dominus noster veniet,
Et pauperum suorum miserebitur. (You heavens, sing for joy,
And earth exults! Our Lord is coming; He will take pity on those
In distress. ......Is 49:13)

Dec 18th – Rex noster adveniet Christus, quem Ioannes praedicavit Agnum
Esse venturum. (Christ Our King is coming, the Lamb whom
John proclaimed.

Dec 19th – Qui venturus est veniet et non tardabit, et iam non erit timor in
Finibus nostris, quoniam ipse est Salvator noster. (He who is to come will not delay; and then there will be no
Fear in our lands, because He is our Savior......
Heb 10:37)

Dec 20th – Egrediatur virga de radice Iesse, et replebitur
          omnis terra
          Gloria Domini, et videbit omnis caro salutare
          Dei.
          (A shoot will spring from Jesse's stock and all
          mankind will see the saving power of God.
          ....See Is 11:1; 40:5; Lk 3:6)

Dec 21st – Modo veniet Dominator Dominus, et vocabitur
          nomen eius
          Emmanuel, quia Nobiscum-Deus. (Soon the Lord
          God will
          Come, and you will call Him Emmanuel, for God
          is with us... See Is 7:14; 8:10)

Dec 22nd – Attolite, portae, capita vestra, et elevamini...et
          introibit rex
          Gloriae. (Gates lift up your heads! Stand erect,
          ancient doors
          And let in the King of Glory. .... Ps 23: 7)

Dec 23rd – Nascetur nobis parvulus, et vocabitur Deus,
          Fortis; in ipso
          Benedicentur omnes tribus terrae. (A little child
          is born for us,
          And he shall be called the mighty God; every
          race on earth shall
          Be blessed in him. .....See Is 9:6; Ps 71:17)

Dec 24th – Ecce iam venit plenitude temporis, in quo misit
          Deus Filium
          Suum in terram. (The appointed time has come;
          God has sent
          His Son into the world......See Gal 4:4)

On to a lighter note. The Texas State fair was loads of fun and we got out of school to boot. There was something special about Elsie the cow. We city kids weren't around animals much. She was always lying in a big bed of hay with those big brown eyes just looking at us. The famous corny dog was the nourishment for the day and to top that off we delved into the cotton candy. You didn't have to be a little kid to ride the merry-go-round. The Ferris wheel and those swings that took you flying out into the air and can't forget the bumper cars. I looked forward to being of age to hop into the roller coaster. The water show was special and of course the museums.

Can you tell I am musing along? I just remembered the ink wells that were carved out of the top corner of our desk at school. The ink bottle got transported back and forth to home along with ink-stained fingers. Then one day the ball point pen showed up on the scene. The first ball point pen debuted at Gimbals in New York, October 29, 1945.

We always printed J.M.J. (Jesus-Mary-Joseph) at the top of our school assignment just like Bishop Sheen did on his TV show "Life Is Worth Living". He printed these letters at the top of his blackboard.

At the end of the school year we would all pile into the bus and head for Vickory Park. It was a great celebration of another successful school year.

Sometime or other we would take a bus ride for a date with culture. The Dallas Symphony Orchestra performed a series of concerts for children. My favorite was "Peter and the Wolf". I loved the lively melody of Peter, played by the string instruments. I could just see him hopping along. Peter's bird friend was played by a flute. When you heard the oboe, you knew it was the duck. The cat was the clarinet sound. The slow deep sound of the bassoon was the grandfather and watch out for the wolf when you heard the French horns.

Periodically, I would go up the street to play at the McRedmond house. They had a bunch of kids like us so I always felt at home. Alice was in my class. We shared a lot of moments on the volleyball and basketball courts.

Lynn lived further on up on Bowser Ave. I loved her upstairs play room with the big window. I was always amazed that she had a lot of crayons to color with. She had a steady supply of that white paste too. We made our paste out of flour and water.

Her mom introduced me to a peanut butter sandwich but not with jelly but you'll never guess. She smeared mayo on top. My eyes got a little wide as I watched her prepare this new concocshon. My first taste was small and slow. I wanted to be polite about the matter. It really is quite delicious.

Across the street from Lynn was Corky's house. His mom played the organ at Church. I thought she was so proficient (as Jane Austin would say) as she accompanied our school choir.

Lillian lived closer to school off Throckmorton. The street car ran right past her house. I would stop by and we played board games mostly clue.

Judy W and I hung out a lot. What good friends we were. We had many discussions about things.

HOLY TRINITY CLASS OF 52'

I had two special boy friends, Buzz and Jimmy, along with all my other friends.

THE 8TH GRADE

My 8th grade classmates were all special to me. I would like to honor them and list them by their first names:

Norman	Judy	ADavid
Jimmy	Corky	Pat C
Gail	Buzz	Lillian
Suzanne	Lynn	Larry
John E	Sandra	Paul
Douglas	Pat L	John L
Doris	Tom M	Judy Mc
Alice	Mary M	Mary N
Sam	Patricia	Gilbert
Mary Fran	Tom R	Henry
Pat S	Robert	Judy W

CLASS SONG OF 52'

We'll remember the time we've spent here,
We'll remember when we're away.
We'll remember the friends we've made here,
And won't forget to come back some day.
We'll remember our dear ole H.T.,
The Priests and the Sisters too.
For we all belong to H.T. and to H.T. we'll all be true.

(The class song was composed by G. Crandall, U. McCaffrey, M. Neuhoff, M.F. Quota, and J Weed.)

Our Principal, Sister Margaret wrote the following:

You have come to one very important milestone in your life's journey and it is well to pause and take note of your achievements and failures. Thanks to a kind Providence, your record is mostly of achievements and very few failures, and it behooves you to give sincere thanks to God for all such benefits.

You have successfully laid the first foundation stone in the triangle of your education, and it is our earnest hope and prayer that you will complete the edifice by attending a Catholic High School and Catholic College.

As you have been so often reminded, you are the future hope of your Church and Country. God has indeed blessed you spiritually and materially, and you should be ever mindful of His admonition: "Unto whom much is given, of him much shall be required."

As you leave the sheltering arms of your beloved Holy Trinity School, we earnestly beg for you the choicest blessings of God the Father and God the Son and God the Holy Spirit.

The dedication of the last issue of "Trinity Topics":

We, the eighth grade students of Holy Trinity, wish to dedicate this last edition of "Trinity Topics" to our assistant Pastor, Father Stack, who has made our school years at Holy Trinity such happy ones.

Due to a serious illness, Father Stack has been in St. Paul's Hospital for several weeks. We have missed his spontaneous laughter and his encouraging words.

We daily send up our prayers for his speedy recovery.

CLASS HISTORY
By Judy Abright

One September morning, eight years ago, quite a few little six-year olds walked hesitatingly into the first grade classroom to be greeted by starry-eyed Sister Gertrude. There is no record of how many little tots cried that day, but I am sure Sister had her hands full... (Of cry- babies)! Eventually, the children settled down, (the girls anyway) then the boys started a series of gang wars with the... (Censored) third graders, which resulted in a disastrous defeat for the latter.

In spite of this, everyone managed to look duly angelic at our First Holy Communion.

In the Second Grade, Lynn D and Judy W were added to the class, while a few pupils dropped out. The gang wars were discontinued due to the reprimand of the good Sisters. That year we enjoyed being old enough to go to the school picnic even though Judy and Lynn got left at the picnic site. Our teacher was Sister Theresa.

The Third Grade rolled around with the highest number of pupils we have ever had....56. Doris came to H.T.S. that year. We encountered the multiplication tables for the first time. Sister De Lourdes had her hands full.

In the Fourth Grade Buzz came back to us. He had been away in the second and third grades. Suzanne, Tommy and Pat L were welcomed additions to our class, as our number had been steadily decreasing. Every morning from 9-10 anyone within a mile could hear us reciting our multiplication tables. This went on for about two weeks, and by that time we were so hoarse that Sister Aurea let us stop.

The Fifth Grade brought us Patty, the traditional tussle with fractions and left us minus one half tooth that Alice broke off when she accidently ran into a basketball post. The boys were initiated into the Altar Boys that year. Sammy spent most of his time running up the radiator pipes.... (We won't tell the reason why Sammy). Sister Mary Angela and her last name was Pera was everybody's favorite. We called her "MAP".

Gail, Mary Frances, Larry and Mary M were our new members in the Sixth Grade....Our losses were very few. I, Judy Abright, ran into the corner of the school building just in time to get my face all scarred up for the trip to Austin. I might also mention that this was the year that Pat S and Tommy R got suspended from our class for a whole week because they were playing "volley ball" with a wad of paper, using a row of heads for a net.

Tommy M, Jim, Norman and Gilbert entered our school in the Seventh Grade. Doris, who had gone to another school during the fifth and sixth grades, came back...but not for long, for she took a two week trip to Cuba during the middle of the year. (We wondered how she rated!) Another addition to our class was a little French boy. Louis, who was born in Algiers, N. Africa. He is not with us now as he had to move to New York. We all still miss him and his quaint accent. Sister Margaret Mary guided us thru this pre teen period.

The outstanding fad in the Seventh Grade was the hand-slapping game. When we started to play it in class one day, Sister Margaret Mary retaliated by making us stand out in the hall and play it from one till three. (Gee, but our hands were sore!)

Now we come to the present...our Eighth Grade!....Sandra joined us in the beginning of the school year, John, who had moved away during the sixth and seventh grades, returned at the end of the term. Sister Veronica ushered us on out into the world of high school.

Naturally most of the excitement this year is concerned with Graduation. In January we measured for our caps and gowns, and in February we ordered our class rings. At the start of this month we began to practice the traditional "Ave Maria" for graduation night. Despite all the excitement of graduation and contemplating our entrance into high school, we all were sad to leave ole H.T.S. and the Sisters who endured our pranks while trying to train us to be good citizens and exemplary Catholics. We can never forget our years at H.T.S.

A MESSAGE FROM OUR PASTOR

My Dear Children,

Vacation days will soon be here. Because you have worked hard the last nine months and the weather is now so hot, you need a rest so that you can come back to school next September healthy and strong for another school year.

What does it mean to have a vacation? It does not mean doing nothing all day or playing all the time. If you are idle very much you will be very unhappy and restless.

You will have much more time for play, but do not play all the time. Spend some of your time helping your mother around the house. Acquire the habit of reading good books. Take a rest in the afternoon. Learn how to make something....perhaps a house for your dog, or a dress for your doll, or a shrine for your statue of our Blessed Mother.

Most important to remember is that there is no vacation from serving God. Don't forget your morning and night prayers. Think of God during the day. Come and visit Him in the Church. Never miss Mass on Sundays unless you are sick. Go to Confession and Holy Communion frequently, and read the book about Our Lord, the Blessed Mother and the Saints.

Take care of yourself. Look both ways before crossing a street. Don't play in the street. Don't ride two on a bike. When you go swimming be sure a life guard is around. Remember God sees you at all times. Have a real good vacation and have lots of fun and May the Blessing of Our Lord be always with you!

Thomas P. Stanton, C.M.

For ole time's sake, I guess I will go ahead and copy this brief report about our girl's baseball team:

The Holy Trinity Girl's Baseball team has started off with a bang! The first game, a thriller with St. Thomas, was a victory for H.T.S. Due to the pitching of Holy Trinity, St. Thomas was held to a score 20 while Holy Trinity ran up a score of 22 runs.

Judy W and Mary M of the eighth grade were the hurlers for H.T. Patty P And Sandra F guarded home plate.

The heroines of the day, however, were the "Home Run Kids" Ursula McC And Frances R of the 7th grade.

Other outstanding feats of play were a spectacular catch by Lillian D and a sommersault over first base by Alice McR.

Really, it was a wonderful game and lots of fun. The girls were happy to have the support of the boys, who attended the game and encouraged us. We appreciate their tips in coaching on the side.

We hope to have another victory at our next game, so come on out and help us to win! (Judy W)

We also had a girl's track team:

At the O.L.G.C. Field Day, our girls made quite a showing. We are proud of all the ribbons they brought home!

Ursula McC. And Alice McR won first place in the three-legged race. Ursula came out second in the sack race, third

169

in the baseball throw and broad jump. Mary M did very well too. She won first place in the 50 yd. dash and in the baseball throw.

Judy W won second place in the 50 yd. dash.

When all the points were totaled, Ursula Mcc came out in second place and Mary M third place. (Judy McK)

Cheer Leaders:

The following cheerleaders received letters last year, so they will get a beautiful megaphone emblem this time.

Ursula McC, Alice McR and Judy W

Our three new cheerleaders will receive letters.

Mary F Q, Betty G and Linda L.

GRADUATION EXERCISES
May 22, 1952

1. Processional	Coronation March
2. Veni Creator Spiritus	Gregorian Chant
3. Sermon	Rev. C.E.Cannon, C.M.
4. Awarding of Diplomas	Very Rev. T.P. Stanton, C.M.
5. Ave Maria	Howard by the Graduates
6. Act of Consecration	Graduates
7. Solemn Benediction	
Celebrant	Very Rev. T.P. Stanton, C.M.
Deacon	Rev. J.N. Thompson, C.M.
Sub-Deacon	Rev. C.E. Cannon, C.M.
8. Adoro Te	Gounod
9. Tantum Ergo	Montani
10. Laudate Domine	Gregorian Chant
11. Praise Ye the Father	Gounod

Music   School Choir

Directed by Miss Rebecca Stiles

Organist – Mrs. Charles Clark

The summer before starting high school, Dad took me for a ride around West Dallas. We talked about the poor and how much Jesus loved them. He asked if I would like to help the Sisters of Charity at Marillac Center teach Bible Study to the little children and I said sure. So off I went setting up the classroom in an old dusty garage. That was a really satisfying experience.

Preparing for High School was another life passage for me anticipating more and more present moments in God's Grace.

HIGH SCHOOL

I'm sitting here at my writing desk in our living room looking out the front windows and across the street at beautiful mimosa trees in full bloom. There is a blue spruce tree off to one side. Looking back at my high school years brings a lot of pure joy. This life passage from grade school to high school was very exciting. So I will start with my memories of Ursuline Academy, Dallas, Texas.

MOTHER AND DAUGHTER – 1956

First of all my sister, JoAnne, was a junior. Her classmates were to become our "big sisters." It seemed to me that everytime I would turn around another "tradition" would unfold. Of course we freshmen had to go through an initiation. We were given this ditty of sorts to memorize as follows:

56ERS FRESHMAN SAYING

Seniors ask "a lowly freshman" _____ "Do you use big words?"

Answer: No, Miss _____ (Senior's name)

In promulgating my esoteric cogitations, or articulating my superficial sentimentalities, philosophical or psychological observations, I beware of platitudinous ponderosity. I let my conversational communications possess a clarified conciseness, a compact comprehensibleness, coalescent consistency, and a concatenated cogency. I let my extemporaneous descanting and unpremeditated expatiations have intelligibility and veracious vivacity, without thrasonical bombast. I acidulously avoid all polysyllabic profundity, pompous prolixity, salacious vacuity, ventriloquial verbosity, and vanilloquent vapidity.

In other words, I talk plainly, briefly, naturally, sensibly, truthfully, purely. I keep from slang; don't put on airs, say what I mean, mean what I say. I don't use big words.

All of the above had to be committed to memory! We had to recognize all seniors and know their names – failure brought consequences!

I liked our uniform, the navy blue suit with the white ship-n-shore blouse, blue bucket hat and to top it off the white gloves for special occasions. Blue and white saddle oxfords with white bobby socks rounded off the outfit.

I was so proud to represent our school especially at the annual Corpus Christi (Body of Christ) procession around the streets of Oak Lawn Ave. Traffic was blocked off as all the Catholic school children participated. Jesus in His Holy Eucharist was placed in a monstrance and reverently carried

173

through the streets. We consider this Blessed Sacrament the source and summit of our Catholic Faith for Jesus is truly present in this Sacrament. Remember as I mentioned before Jesus said this IS My Body. He didn't say this looks like My Body.

EILEEN – ANGELA – URSULA

The Knights of Columbus marched on either side of the Priest as he carried Jesus along. My father was one of those Knights. This reminds me that each time dad had to put on his tucks for a Knight's celebration, he was always missing one or two of those little black studs. There was mom rushing around trying to find them. I don't doubt that occasionally he carried on without them. No problem. After all he always had his mind and heart on more serious matters.

Thinking about the academic part of school, I was no scholar. I can remember dad calling me in several days before I was to register for classes. He said, "Young lady, you are going to take four years of Latin, aren't you?" Oh, I am? "Yes indeed you are." So off I went telling myself that after all Latin was the official language of our Church. The first six weeks grade was a whopping D and I knew that I better get with the program. I brought the grade up to a B and then cruised thru with Cs. I also took two years of Spanish and really enjoyed learning this language.

Now, as you know, math was required. First year algebra wasn't so bad. I enjoyed the logic required to work the problems. Second year geometry was the pits with all those angles. I thought a person has to be some kind of space cadet to maneuver around those angles. It is quite amazing to me that I passed this course and all the rest for that matter. You see I spent time helping my brothers and sisters and my mom with various and sundry duties. I didn't have a lot of time for study which really was fine with me after all.

English classes were my favorite. There was something melodious with words and their meaning. Book reports were a problem as I somehow didn't have time to read a book from cover to cover. Thank God for the cliff notes and discussions with my classmates.

Music seemed to fill my soul. Joining the school choir was pure joy. I could hear a song one time and by rote know it. I sang alto.

Sometime during these years I took a course in Logic. It was taught by Mother Adelaide. This skill has remained with me to this day. The transition from premises to conclusion, the logical connection between them, is the inference upon which the argument relies – all those syllogisms!

I'm still sitting here just musing. I'll be writing about what

175

comes to me. I remember I got my hair cut real short in my freshman year. I was the first in my class to do so. It provided me a simple style that didn't take a lot of time. I was too busy about many other important matters to bother with my hair.

THE SHORT BOB

I loved the Friday night dances at Jesuit. My entire self was absorbed in the rhythm of the music. When the bop came on the scene, I was not a bit bashful to go with it. Even to this day, just play some music and my foot starts tapping. Mr. Thomas, S.J. organized a square dance club with some of us Ursuline girls. We practiced at Jesuit. What fun!

If you don't mind, I would like to mention more about my friend Fr. Rick Thomas, S.J. (God rest his soul) For his ordination to the Priesthood I made the long white linen cloth he used to wrap around his hands. Later he sent me this cloth. For many years he was at a mission in El Paso, Texas. For Thanksgiving, his people would prepare a large meal, cross the border into Mexico and distribute the food. Once many more people showed up and at the start it didn't look like they had enough food. Fr. Rick said not to worry. He blessed the food and it multiplied! Everyone was fed with left over's. Praise God for that miracle.

Moving along now, I need to mention athletics. I was blessed with a strong coordinated body. Any sport, no matter which one, was easy to start with and perfected with practice. Because I was so into the present moment the focus was 100% on what I was doing at the time.

Back in my time we served the volleyball underhanded. I had such power in my serve that the ball would barely skim over the top of the net and skip across open fingers and out racking up another point for my team.

Basketball season rolled around next. If you would drop by my house I would likely be out back practicing with some of my boy friends. I can't remember any of my girl friends joining me in a round of play.

During football season, no I didn't suit up, but Skip and I would be out front, he on one side of the street and me on the other. We would kick that ball back and forth. I got to where I managed a nice spiral kick. During baseball season I would pad the catcher's mitt to ease the burn of one of Skip's fast balls. We played tennis on our own. I had a mean back hand. Joanne and I would volley the ball out front in the street. At times we would bicycle to that tennis court over on Douglas.

Summer sports eased up by my junior year in high school. When I turned 16 I got a job on weekends and holidays at the old St Paul Hospital on Hall St. Like my sister, Joanne, before me, we worked in the business office manually sorting patient charges at .75/hr. We signed over our paychecks to our dad and were happy to do so. By the way I was working one Sunday in the fall of 1955 when I got a call from Jesuit informing me that I would be the Homecoming Queen from Ursuline. What a surprise that was! More about this later.

I so enjoyed the dances at the Knight of Columbus Hall. They were on a Friday night. The dances were divided up between the Junior Youth and the Senior Youth. Music was provided by "Don Clark's Orchestra" and "The Crowns". Jimmy Begg was the M.C... The grand finale was always "God Bless America".

Janis, Fran, Judy A and I performed some songs. Sue and Judy W opened the entertainment with a dance. The highlight of the evening was the specialty tap dancers.

In my junior year at one of these dances, some guy danced a lot with me. He was already in college. He asked me out and I flat out told him I was too young but that I had an older sister and she's real pretty. I gave him our phone number in case he was interested. I don't remember if he called or not.

Along this socializing theme, I was invited to an Aggie football game once and my father refused to let me go. Not until later did I find out that the young ladies get a kiss from their aggie date after every touchdown. It's a tradition! My dad was not about to let this daughter go thru that routine. I probably wouldn't have minded one little bit as the score of that game was 20-7 in favor of the Aggies.

Another time my sisters Angela and Eileen had some of their boyfriends over. It was summer. I was out back reading in the hammock. My dad came home and noticed me there. He called me in to inform me that I was not to lounge in the hammock, especially in shorts, while young men were around. I thought, gosh they're not my boy friends. I understood what he meant so I changed into a skirt.

My dad had strict rules for us girls. We had to attend school sponsored dances with a group until we turned 16 when we could go on a "date". Oh brother and if he noticed us dating any one guy in particular, he would have a discussion with us about "going steady". Thank goodness I didn't have to worry about this as I had lots of guys asking me out.

I want to mention one guy, Dick, who lived in Oak Cliff. He was tall and lanky with dark hair and brown eyes. We had moved out to N. Dallas. One Sunday afternoon, my brothers and sisters came running into my room to let me know that they could see Dick, from the upstairs window, walking down Merrell Rd. carrying a bird cage. He brought me a little yellow canary. How sweet was that? Dick left high school and joined the navy. In my senior year I wrote him a "Dear John letter", informing him that I was leaving home to dedicate my life in the service to my Church. I think I broke his heart but I sure didn't mean to.

I want to take a moment and remember our Principal, Mother Delores Marie, O.S.U. She was a mother to us in more ways than one. She was Johnny on the spot and never missed a trick. She had that look of discipline and did not tolerate the foolishness of pranks, being late to class or wearing a sloppy uniform. I will never forget her humor. She had a broad smile and you just knew everything was going to be all right after all.

MOTHER DELORES MARIE, O.S.U.

I will interject here the "prank" we pulled on Miss Hines, our music teacher. One day, Miss Hines asked us for our phone numbers in case she needed to contact us away from school.

Someone, I can't remember who, quickly whispered for us to start switching our phone numbers with each other. Sure enough, several evenings later, Miss Hines needed to call so-in-so but got another so-in-so instead. It wasn't long when she realized the situation. It wasn't long either when we saw the angry side of Mother Delores Marie. I'm sure we were punished in some way but I don't remember how. I know an apology to Miss Hines was in order from each one of us.

Miss Hines taught us a poem by Gerard Manley Hopkins (1844-1889),

"Mary Mother of Divine Grace Compared to the Air We Breathe".

It's a very long poem so I would like to quote some of it. To save space I will put it in narrative form.

Wild air, world-mothering air, nestling me everywhere, that each eyelash or hair girdles; goes home betwixt the fleeciest, frailest-fixed snow flake; that's fairly mixed with riddles, and is rife in every least thing's life; This needful, never spent and nursing element; my more than meat and drink, my meal at every wink' this air which by life's law my lung must draw and draw now, but to breathe it's praise, minds me in many ways of her who not only gave God infinity, dwindles to infancy, welcome in womb and breast, birth milk, and all the rest, but mothers each new grace, that does now reach our race, Mary Immaculate, merely a woman, yet whose presence, power is great as no goddess's was deemed, dreamed; who this one work has to do – Let all God's glory through, God's glory, which would go thru' her and from her flow off, and no way but so. ....If I have understood she holds high motherhood towards all our ghostly good, and plays in grace her part about man's beating heart............Again look overhead how air is azured. O how! Nay do but stand where you can lift your hand skywards: rich, rich it laps round the four finger-gaps. ......So God was God of old; a mother came to mould those limbs like ours which are what must make our daystar much dearer to mankind.... Be thou then, O thou dear mother, my atmosphere; my happier world wherein to wend and meet no sin; Above me, round me lie fronting my forward eye with sweet and scarless sky; stir in my ears, speak there of God's love, O live air, of patience, penance, prayer; World-mothering air, air wild, wound with thee, is thee isled, fold home, fast fold thy child.

I know Mother Delores Marie had a big role in planning the move of Ursuline Academy to the new campus on Walnut Hill Lane in N. Dallas in 1951.

I would like to give a brief synopsis of Ursuline Academy in Dallas, Texas:

February 2, 1874 – Ursuline opened it's doors as a school for 7 young women in a small four-room cottage.

1876 – Two-story wooden struction for school and convent.

1882 – First unit of Ursuline on St. Joseph Farm – located on Bryan, Live Oak and Haskell Streets.

1889 – Second unit – used as a Provincialate

1902 – Third Unit – Day and boarders quarters

1910 – Chapel and auditorium

1921 – Novitiate

1942 – bought property on Walnut Hill Lane – used Merici residence for high school

1951 – new Academy (High School and Elementary) and convent

1956 – Gym/Auditorium and separate elementary building

1963 – bought Sailer property

1964 – Kindergarten building

1971 – Art Building

1974 – Sister's Residence

1977 – Major renovation in High School

1983 – Dining/Arts complex – Haggar Center

1984 – Beatrice M Haggerty Library

There continues to be additions and improvemts to this hollowed institution of learning. I will mention that Ursuline opened one of the city's first kindergartens as part of the academy's program in 1918. The grammar school was discontinued in 1976.

Back in those days, the blue and gold bows were prestigious honors conferred for outstanding deportment and academics. It took me 4 years to finally earn a blue bow. Never you mind the gold bow. That was an unattainable goal because high academic achievement was not on my agenda.

It's been several months since writing more about high school. You see Bill Rosenfeld, a retired editor here in Mountain Home, was assisting me with this project and he died suddenly. He was very kind and encouraged me in this venture. He told me to say a little prayer each day before starting to write and so I have. Once when he dropped by, I asked him, "Bill, you're not going to be changing my words are you?" He smiled and said he wouldn't think of it. After all this is my story and I am writing from my heart. He did say he would make a grammatical correction if indicated. I understood that. So now I will continue this story remembering the kind gentleman who got me started.

I'm going to write about my calling to the Religious Life. It all started when I was 9 years old. Yes I knew back then that Jesus wanted me to serve Him in this special way. I also knew that He wanted me to live in the present moments of each stage of my life. Indeed I so enjoyed all the years leading up to my senior year in high school. Sometime before this, two Medical Mission Sisters came to our school to talk about their role in serving the sick in foreign missions. Oh! How interesting! I knew for sure that I wanted to care for the sick, that I could see Jesus in each soul that I would touch. It didn't take me long to lock in the two, care of the sick and in a foreign land.

In the autumn of my senior year we had a senior retreat. Fr Weber, S.J. was the retreat master. I discussed my decision with him and received encouragement. I had no doubts. Fr Weber must have been overwhelmed because several more of my classmates also had vocations to the Religious Life. I told my parents after this retreat but wanted to wait before sharing the news with my brothers and sisters.

I decided to tell the rest of the family around Christmas

time. We called everybody into the living room. I made sure a box of Kleenex was handy as I just knew my sisters would need it. Sure enough some tears flowed. Angela told me later that after I left home she and Eileen were mad at God for taking their sister away. One Sunday they did not want to go to Church but dad smoothed over their feelings.

CLASS DAY – 1956

Since I'm writing about the autumn of my senior year I'll write more about the Jesuit Homecoming Celebration. As I mentioned before I got the call while at work at St Paul's Hospital. I was to represent Ursuline as the Queen of Homecoming and Mary was to be the Princess. That was a big surprise for me. It was fun preparing for the big night. I kept in touch with Jesus throughout. As we were driven around the football stadium in a convertible waving at the crowds, I was talking to Jesus and making this a joyous prayer. He meant more to me really than all this glitter. I found myself thinking of Him whenever I heard a love song.

I so enjoyed preparing for high school graduation and the traditional class day ceremony donning the white formal gown, the white hat and carrying those beautiful red roses. I was in step with my older sister, Joanne, and before her my Mother and aunts who wore similar attire.

GRADUATION !

The night of my graduation from high school mom and dad took me to Jay's Marine Grill. "Young lady, you may order a highball if you wish, you are now of age," my father said. Well, how exciting! I ordered a 7 & 7. You know something? I really didn't like the stuff, but was glad to participate in this life passage event.

The events of the spring semester unfolded as I prepared to leave home for this new life in Christ. I plan to write a separate story on this part of my life as my mother saved 110 of my letters from Africa.

Before I sign off, I would like to honor my classmates and mention their names:

CLASS OF 1956

Dee	Eva	Janis
Mary N	Rosalyn	Virginia (Rest in Peace)
Patricia C	Fran	Jean
Diane	Lynn	Joann
Patricia H	Barbara	Ann M
Mary Edith	Sue	Patsy
Judy W	Ann B	Suzanne (Rest in Peace)
Vickie	Margaret Ann	Alice (Rest in Peace)
Sherry	Teresa	Judy A
Mike	Sheila	Doris
Rosemary		

Patsy was our class President, Diane the Vice-President, Lynn the Secretary, and Jean the Treasurer. Our class colors were yellow and brown.

There were parties and luncheons to celebrate the big day. Our class went out to Texoma to the Trails End Lodge and everybody had a time clearing their beds of potato chips and bugs. I remember how happy I was to have my parents join me for the class banquet. Somehow I was nominated as the most courteous. The commencement ceremony took place at Fair Park Auditorium on May 23, 1956. Dr. Kenneth Brasted, President of Dallas University, gave the address.

For ole time sake I will list the caption in our senior yearbook:

URSULA MCCAFFREY: Honor Graduate; Sodality 2,3,4; Glee Club 1,2,3,4, Secretary 1,3; Athletic Council 1,2,3,4, Secretary 4; Varsity Volleyball 1,2,3,4, Captain 4; Varsity Basketball 1,2; Class Teams 1,2,3,4, Captain; Homecoming Queen 4.

A heart warming laugh.....agile.....self-sacrificing...."Come on y'all.....Ursula

Printed in the United States
by Baker & Taylor Publisher Services